CREATURES FROM BEYOND

CREATURES FROM BEYOND

NINE STORIES OF SCIENCE FICTION AND FANTASY

edited by

Terry Carr

THOMAS NELSON INC., PUBLISHERS

Nashville • *New York*

ACKNOWLEDGMENTS

THE WORM by David H. Keller. Copyright 1927 by E. P. Company, Inc. From *Amazing Stories,* by permission of Scott Meredith Literary Agency, Inc., 580 Fifth Ave., New York, N.Y. 10036.

MIMIC by Donald A. Wollheim. Copyright 1942 by Fictioneers, Inc. From *Astonishing Stories,* by permission of the author.

IT by Theodore Sturgeon. Copyright 1940 by Street & Smith Publications, Inc. From *Unknown,* by permission of the author.

BEAUTY AND THE BEAST by Henry Kuttner. Copyright 1940 by Better Publications, Inc. From *Thrilling Wonder Stories,* by permission of the Harold Matson Co., Inc.

SOME ARE BORN CATS by Terry and Carol Carr. Copyright © 1973 by Rand McNally & Co. From *Science Fiction Tales,* by permission of the authors.

FULL SUN by Brian W. Aldiss. Copyright © 1967 by Damon Knight. From *Orbit 2,* by permission of the author.

THE SILENT COLONY by Robert Silverberg. Copyright 1954 by Columbia Publications, Inc. From *Future Science Fiction,* by permission of the author and his agents, Scott Meredith Literary Agency, Inc., 580 Fifth Ave., New York, N.Y. 10036.

THE STREET THAT WASN'T THERE by Clifford D. Simak and Carl Jacobi. Copyright 1941 by H-K Publications, Inc. From *Comet Stories,* by permission of Robert P. Mills Ltd.

DEAR DEVIL by Eric Frank Russell. Copyright 1950 by Clark Publishing Co. From *Other Worlds,* by permission of the author and his agents, Scott Meredith Literary Agency, Inc., 580 Fifth Ave., New York, N.Y. 10036.

CONTENTS

INTRODUCTION
I

THE WORM
David H. Keller
3

MIMIC
Donald A. Wollheim
21

IT
Theodore Sturgeon
29

BEAUTY AND THE BEAST
Henry Kuttner
59

SOME ARE BORN CATS
Terry and Carol Carr
79

FULL SUN
Brian W. Aldiss
95

THE SILENT COLONY
Robert Silverberg
III

THE STREET THAT WASN'T THERE
Clifford D. Simak and Carl Jacobi
117

DEAR DEVIL
Eric Frank Russell
137

CREATURES FROM BEYOND

INTRODUCTION

Human imagination has always been captured by the idea of what strange creatures may lie in waiting, somewhere beyond our ken—in the dark outside our caves, in the uncharted depths of the seas, in the infinite reaches of space.

After all, the history of humanity hasn't always been one of brave, inquisitive explorers making discoveries—sometimes it was we who were discovered, by powerful predatory beasts forced to range beyond their former hunting grounds, or by strange birds like explosions of color in the air as they migrated to winter quarters.

The unexpected is always dramatic, the unknown always fascinating. And so our literature from the earliest times is filled with tales of dragons, rocs, unicorns, and sea serpents. In modern times, science fiction has looked out into space for strange beings, whether deadly marauders like the Martians of H. G. Wells' *The War of the Worlds* or mysterious, almost godlike beings such as in Clarke and Kubrick's *2001*.

We still wonder: Are there creatures somewhere who are watching us? What might their purpose be? And what if they come to Earth?

Here is a collection of stories about such Creatures from Beyond, as imagined by some of the top writers of modern fantasy and science fiction.

—*Terry Carr*

THE WORM

David H. Keller

We pride ourselves on having explored our planet, but at best we've only scratched the surface—quite literally, for the vast interior of Earth is still almost wholly unknown to us. What creatures might dwell there, burrowing inexorably through ancient rock? And if one of those creatures should come up to the surface, what then?

David H. Keller was one of the most influential writers in the early days of science fiction; trained as a psychiatrist, he concentrated on human emotions in his stories. As a result, stories such as "The Worm," which he wrote nearly fifty years ago, are still powerful and moving.

The miller patted his dog on the head, as he whispered: "We are going to stay here. Our folks, your ancestors and mine, have been here for nearly two hundred years, and queer it would be to leave now because of fear."

The gristmill stood, a solid stone structure, in an isolated Vermont valley. Years ago every day had been a busy one for the mill and the miller, but now only the mill wheel was busy. There was no grist for the mill and no one lived in the valley. Blackberries and hazel grew where once the pastures had been green. The hand of time had passed over the farms and the only folk left were sleeping in the churchyard. A family of squirrels nested in the pulpit, while on the tombstones silent snails left their cryptic messages in silvery streaks. Thompson's Valley was being handed back to nature. Only the old bachelor miller, John Staples, remained. He was too proud and too stubborn to do anything else.

The mill was his home, even as it had served all of his family for a home during the last two hundred years. The first Staples had built it to stay, and it was still as strong as on the day it was finished. There was a basement for the machinery of the mill, the first floor was the place of grinding and storage, and the upper two floors served as the Staples homestead. The building was warm in winter and cool in summer. Times past it had sheltered a dozen Stapleses at a time; now it provided a home for John Staples and his dog.

He lived there with his books and his memories. He had no friends and desired no associates. Once a year he went to the nearest town and bought supplies of all kinds, paying for them in gold. It was supposed that he was wealthy. Rumor credited him with being a miser. He attended to his own business, asked the world to do the same, and on a winter's evening laughed silently over Burton and Rabelais, while his dog chased rabbits in his heated sleep upon the hearth.

The winter of 1935 was beginning to threaten the valley, but with an abundance of food and wood in the mill, the recluse looked forward to a comfortable period of desuetude. No matter how cold the weather, he was warm and contented. With the inherent ability of his family, he had been able to convert the waterpower into electricity. When the wheel was frozen, he used the electricity stored in his storage batteries. Every day he puttered around among the machinery, which it was his pride to keep in perfect order. He assured the dog that if business ever did come to the mill, he would be ready for it.

It was on Christmas Day of that winter that he first heard the noise. Going down to the basement to see that nothing had been injured by the bitter freeze of the night before, his attention was attracted, even while descending the stone steps, by a peculiar grinding noise that seemed to come from out of the ground. His ancestors, building for permanency, had not only put in solid foundations, but had paved the entire basement with slate flagstones three feet wide and as many inches thick. Between these the dust of two centuries had gathered and hardened.

Once his feet were on this pavement, Staples found that he could not only hear the noise, but he could also feel the vibrations that accompanied it through the flagstones. Even through his heavy leather boots he could feel the rhythmic pulsations. Pulling off his mittens, he stooped over and put his fingertips on the stone. To his surprise it was warm in spite of the fact that the temperature had been below zero the night before. The vibration was more distinct to his fingertips than it had been to his feet. Puzzled, he threw himself on the slate stone and put his ear to the warm surface.

The sound he now heard made him think of the grinding of the millstones when he was a boy and the farmers had brought corn to be ground into meal. There had been no cornmeal ground in the mill for fifty years, yet here was the sound of stone scraping slowly and regularly on stone. He could not understand it. In fact it was some time before he tried to explain it. With the habit born of years of solitary thinking, he first collected all the available facts about this noise. He knew that during the long winter evenings he would have time enough to do his thinking.

Going to his sitting room, he secured a walking stick of ash and went back to the cellar. Holding the handle of the cane lightly, he placed the other end on a hundred different spots on the floor, and each time he held it long enough to determine the presence or absence of vibration. To his surprise he found that while it varied in strength, it was present all over the cellar with the exception of the four corners. The maximum intensity was about in the center.

That evening he concentrated on the problem before him. He had been told by his grandfather that the mill was built on solid rock. As a young man he had helped clean out a well near the mill and recalled that, instead of being dug out of gravel or dirt, it had the appearance of being drilled out of solid granite. There was no difficulty in believing that the earth under the mill was also solid rock. There was no reason for thinking otherwise. Evidently some of these strata of stone had become loose and were slipping and twisting under the mill. The simplest explanation was the most reasonable: it was simply a geological phenomenon. The behavior of the dog, however, was not so easily explained. He had refused to go with his master into the cellar, and now, instead of sleeping in comfort before the fire, he was in an attitude of strained expectancy. He did not bark, or even whine, but crept silently to his master's chair, looking at him anxiously.

The next morning the noise was louder. Staples heard it in his bed, and at first he thought that some bold adventurer had come into the forest and was sawing down a tree. That was what it sounded like, only softer and longer in its rhythm. Buzzzzzz—Buzzzzzz—Buzzzzzzz. The dog, distinctly unhappy, jumped up on the bed and crawled uneasily so he could nuzzle the man's hand.

Through the four legs of the bed, Staples could feel the same vibration that had come to him through the handle of his cane the day before. That made him think. The vibration was now powerful enough to be appreciated, not through a walking stick, but through the walls of the building. The noise could be heard as well on the third floor as in the cellar.

He tried to fancy what it sounded like—not what it was—but what it was like. The first idea had been that it resembled a saw going through oak; then came the thought of bees swarming, only these were large bees and millions of them; but finally all he could think of was the grinding of stones in a gristmill, the upper stone against the lower; and now the sound was Grrrrrrrr—Grrrrrrrr instead of Bzzzzzz or Hummmmmmm.

That morning he took longer than usual to shave and was more methodical than was his wont in preparing breakfast for himself and the dog. It seemed as though he knew that some-time he would have to go down into the cellar but wanted to postpone it as long as he could. In fact, he finally put on his coat and beaver hat and mittens and walked outdoors before he went to the basement. Followed by the dog, who seemed happy for the first time in hours, he walked out on the frozen ground and made a circle around the building he called his home. Without knowing it, he was trying to get away from the noise, to go somewhere he could walk without feeling that peculiar tingling.

Finally he went into the mill and started down the steps to the cellar. The dog hesitated on the top step, went down two steps and then jumped back to the top step, where he started to whine. Staples went steadily down the steps, but the dog's behavior did not add to his peace of mind. The noise was much louder than it was the day before, and he did not need a cane to detect the vibration—the whole building was shak-ing. He sat down on the third step from the bottom and thought the problem over before he ventured out on the floor. He was especially interested in an empty barrel that was dancing around the middle of the floor.

The power of the millwheel was transferred through a sim-ple series of shafts, cogs, and leather belting to the grinding elements on the first floor. All this machinery for transmitting power was in the basement. The actual grinding had been done on the first floor. The weight of all this machinery, as well as of the heavy millstones on the first floor, was carried entirely by the flooring of the basement. The ceiling of the first floor was built on long pine beams that stretched across the entire building and were sunk into the stone walls at ei-ther side.

Staples started to walk around on the slate flagstones when he observed something that made him decide to stay on the steps. The floor was beginning to sink in the middle; not much, but enough to cause some of the shafts to separate from the ceiling. The ceiling seemed to sag. He saw that light objects like the empty barrel were congregating at the middle of the cellar. There was not much light but he was easily able to see that the floor was no longer level; that it was becoming saucer-shaped. The grinding noise grew louder. The steps he sat on were of solid masonry, stoutly connected with and a part of the wall. These shared in the general vibration. The whole building began to sing like a cello.

One day he had been to the city and heard an orchestra play. He had been interested in the large violins, especially the one that was so large the player had to stay on his feet to play it. The feeling of the stone step under him reminded him of the notes of this violin the few times it had been played by itself. He sat there. Suddenly he started, realizing that in a few more minutes he would be asleep. He was not frightened but in some dim way he knew he must not go to sleep—not here. Whistling, he ran up the steps to get his electric torch. With that in his hand, he went back to the steps. Aided by the steady light, he saw that several large cracks had appeared in the floor and that some of the stones, broken loose from their fellows, were moving slowly in a drunken, meaningless way. He looked at his watch. It was only a little after nine.

And then the noise stopped.

No more noise! No more vibration! Just a broken floor and every bit of the machinery of the mill disabled and twisted. In the middle of the floor was a hole where one of the pavement stones had dropped through. Staples carefully walked across and threw the light down this hole. Then he lay down and carefully put himself in such a position that he could look down the hole. He began to sweat. There did not seem to be any bottom!

Back on the solid steps, he tried to give that hole its proper value. He could not understand it, but he did not need the whining of the dog to tell him what to do. That hole must be closed as soon as possible.

Like a flash, the method of doing so came to him. On the floor above he had cement. There were hundreds of grain sacks. Water was plentiful in the millrace. All that day he worked, carefully closing the hole with a great stopper of bags and wire. Then he placed timbers above and finally covered it all with cement, rich cement. Night came and he still worked. Morning came and still he staggered down the steps, each time with a bag of crushed stone or cement on his shoulder, or with two buckets of water in his hands. At noon the next day the floor was no longer concave but convex. On top of the hole was four feet of timbers, bags and concrete. Then and only then did he go and make some coffee. He drank it, cup after cup, and slept.

The dog stayed on the bed at his feet.

When the man woke, the sun was streaming in through the windows. It was a new day. Though the fire had long since died out, the room was warm. Such days in Vermont were called weather breeders. Staples listened. There was no sound except the ticking of his clock. Not realizing what he was doing, he knelt by the bed, thanked God for His mercies, jumped into bed again and slept for another twenty-four hours. This time he awoke and listened. There was no noise. He was sure that by this time the cement had hardened. This morning he stayed awake and shared a Gargantuan meal with the dog. Then it seemed the proper thing to go to the basement. There was no doubt that the machinery was a wreck, but the hole was closed. Satisfied that the trouble was over, he took his gun and dog and went hunting.

When he returned, he did not have to enter the mill to

know that the grinding had begun again. Even before he started down the steps, he recognized too well the vibration and the sound. This time it was a melody of notes, a harmony of discords, and he realized that the thing, which before had cut through solid rock, was now wearing its way through a cement in which were bags, timbers and pieces of iron. Each of these gave a different tone. Together they all wailed over their dissolution.

Staples saw, even with first glance, that it would not be long before his cement "cork" would be destroyed. What was there to do next? All that day when hunting, his mind had been dimly working on that problem. Now he had the answer. He could not cork the hole, so he would fill it with water. The walls of the mill were solid, but he could blast a hole through them and turn the millrace into the cellar. The race, fed by the river, took only a part of what it could take, if its level were rapidly lowered. Whatever it was that was breaking down the floor of the mill could be drowned. If it was alive, it could be killed. If it was fire, it could be quenched. There was no use to wait until the hole was again opened. The best plan was to have everything ready. He went back to his kitchen and cooked a meal of ham and eggs. He ate all he could. He boiled a pot of coffee. Then he started to work. The wall reached three feet down below the surface. A charge of powder, heavy enough to break through, would wreck the whole building, so he began to peck at the wall, like a bird pecking at a nut. First a period of drilling and then a little powder and a muffled explosion. A few buckets of loosened rock. Then some more drilling and another explosion. At last he knew that only a few inches of rock lay between the water and the cellar.

All this time there had been a symphony of noises, a disharmony of sounds. The constant grinding came from the floor, interrupted with the sound of sledge or crowbar, dull explosion of powder, and crashing of rock fragments on the floor. Staples worked without stop save to drink coffee. The dog stood on the upper steps.

Then, without warning, the whole floor caved in. Staples jumped to the steps. These held. On the first day there had been a hole a few feet wide. Now the opening occupied nearly the entire area of the floor. Staples, nauseated, looked down to the bottom. There, about twenty feet below him, a mass of rocks and timbers churned in a peculiar way, but all gradually disappeared in a second hole, fifteen feet wide. Even as he looked they all disappeared in this median hole.

The opening he had been breaking in the wall was directly across from the steps. There was a charge of powder but no way of going across to light the fuse. Still there was no time to lose and he had to think fast. Running to the floor above he picked up his rifle and went to the bottom of the steps. He was able to throw the beam from his searchlight directly into the hole in the wall. Then he shot—once—twice, and the third time the explosion told him he had succeeded.

The water started to run into the cellar. Not fast at first but more rapidly as the mud and weeds were cleared out. Finally an eight-inch stream flowed steadily into the bottomless hole. Staples sat on the bottom steps. Soon he had the satisfaction of seeing the water fill the larger hole and then cover the floor, what there was left of it. In another hour he had to leave the lower steps. He went out to the millrace and saw that there was still enough water to fill a hundred such holes. A deep sense of satisfaction filled his weary mind.

And again, after eating, he sought sleep.

When he awoke, he heard the rain angrily tapping at the windows with multi-fingers. The dog was on the woven rug by the side of the bed. He was still restless and seemed pleased to have his master awake. Staples dressed more warmly than usual and spent an extra half hour making pancakes to eat with honey. Sausages and coffee helped assuage his hunger. Then with rubber boots and a heavy raincoat, he went out into the valley. The very first thing that he noticed was the millrace. It was practically empty. The little stream of water at the bottom was pouring into the hole he had blasted into the stone wall hours before. The race had contained eight feet of water. Now barely six inches remained, and the dread came to the man that the hole in the cellar was not only emptying the race but was also draining the little river that for thousands of years had flowed through the valley. It had never gone dry. He hastened over to the dam and his worst fears were realized. Instead of a river, there was simply a streak of mud with cakes of dirty ice, all being washed by the torrent of rain. With relief he thought of this rain. Millions of tons of snow would melt and fill the river. Ultimately the hole would fill and the water would rise again in the millrace. Still he was uneasy. What if the hole had no bottom?

When he looked into the basement he was little reassured. The water was still going down, though slowly. It was rising in the basement and this meant that it was now running in faster than it was running down.

Leaving his coat and boots on the first floor, he ran up the stone steps to the second floor, built a fire in the living room and started to smoke—and think. The machinery of the mill was in ruins; of course it could be fixed, but as there was no more need of it, the best thing was to leave it alone. He had gold saved by his ancestors. He did not know how much, but he could live on it. Restlessly he reviewed the past week, and, unable to rest, hunted for occupation. The idea of the gold stayed in his mind and the final result was that he again put on his boots and coat and carried the entire treasure to a little dry cave in the woods about a half mile from the mill. Then he came back and started to cook his dinner. He went past the cellar door three times without looking down.

Just as he and the dog had finished eating, he heard a noise. It was a different one this time, more like a saw going through wood, but the rhythm was the same: Hrrrrr—Hrrrrr.

He started to go to the cellar but this time he took his rifle, and though the dog followed, he howled dismally with his tail between his legs, shivering.

As soon as Staples reached the first floor, he felt the vibration. Not only could he feel the vibration, he could see it. It seemed that the center of the floor was being pushed up. Flashlight in hand, he opened the cellar door. There was no water there now—in fact there was no cellar left! In front of him was a black wall on which the light played in undulating waves. It was a wall and it was moving. He touched it with the end of his rifle. It was hard and yet there was a give to it. Feeling the rock, he could feel it move. Was it alive? Could there be a living rock? He could not see around it but he felt that the bulk of the thing filled the entire cellar and was pressing against the ceiling. That was it! The thing was boring through the first floor. It had destroyed and filled the cellar! It had swallowed the river! Now it was working at the first floor. If this continued, the mill was doomed. Staples knew that it was a thing alive and *he had to stop it!*

He was thankful that all of the steps in the mill were of stone, fastened and built into the wall. Even though the floor did fall in, he could still go to the upper rooms. He realized that from now on the fight had to be waged from the top floors. Going up the steps, he saw that a small hole had been cut through the oak flooring. Even as he watched, this grew larger. Trying to remain calm, realizing that only by doing so could he retain his sanity, he sat down in a chair and timed the rate of enlargement. But there was no need of using a watch: the hole grew larger—and larger and larger—and now he began to see the dark hole that had sucked the river dry. Now it was three feet in diameter—now four feet—now six. It was working smoothly now—it was not only grinding—*but it was eating.*

Staples began to laugh. He wanted to see what it would do when the big stone grinders slipped silently down into that maw. That would be a rare sight. All well enough to swallow a few pavement stones, but when it came to a twenty-ton grinder, that would be a different kind of a pill. "I hope you choke!" The walls hurled back the echo of his shouts and frightened him into silence. Then the floor began to tilt and the chairs to slide toward the opening. Staples sprang toward the steps.

"Not yet!" he shrieked. "Not today, Elenora! Some other day, but not today!" And then from the safety of the steps, he witnessed the final destruction of the floor and all in it. The stones slipped down, the partitions, the beams, and then, as though satisfied with the work and the food, the Thing dropped down, down, down and left Staples dizzy on the steps looking into a hole, dark, deep, coldly bottomless surrounded by the walls of the mill, and below them a circular hole cut out of the solid rock. On one side a little stream of water came through the blasted wall and fell, a tiny waterfall, below. Staples could not hear it splash at the bottom.

Nauseated and vomiting, he crept up the steps to the second floor, where the howling dog was waiting for him. On the floor he lay, sweating and shivering in dumb misery. It took hours for him to change from a frightened animal to a cerebrating god, but ultimately he accomplished even this, cooked some more food, warmed himself and slept.

And while he dreamed, the dog kept sleepless watch at his feet. He awoke the next morning. It was still raining, and Staples knew that the snow was melting on the hills and soon would change the little valley river into a torrent. He wondered whether it was all a dream, but one look at the dog showed him the reality of the last week. He went to the second floor again and cooked breakfast. After he had eaten, he slowly went down the steps. That is, he started to go, but halted at the sight of the hole. The steps had held and ended on a wide stone platform. From there another flight of steps went down to what had once been the cellar. Those two flights of steps clinging to the walls had the solid stonemill on one side, but on the inside they faced a chasm, circular in outline and seemingly bottomless; but the man knew there was a bottom and from that pit the Thing had come—and would come again.

That was the horror of it. He was so certain that it would come again. Unless he was able to stop it. How could he? Could he destroy a Thing that was able to bore a thirty-foot hole through solid rock, swallow a river and digest grinding stones like so many pills? One thing he was sure of—he could accomplish nothing without knowing more about it. To know more, he had to watch. He determined to cut a hole through the floor. Then he could see the Thing when it came up. He cursed himself for his confidence, but he was sure it would come.

It did. He was on the floor looking into the hole he had sawed through the plank, and he saw it come: but first he heard it. It was a sound full of slithering slidings, wrathful rasping of rock against rock—but, no! That could not be, for this Thing was alive. Could this be rock and move and grind and eat and drink? Then he saw it come into the cellar and finally to the level of the first floor, and then he saw its head and face.

The face looked at the man and Staples was glad that the hole in the floor was as small as it was. There was a central mouth filling half the space; fully fifteen feet in diameter was that mouth, and the sides were ashen gray and quivering. There were no teeth.

That increased the horror: a mouth without teeth, without any visible means of mastication, and yet Staples shivered as he thought of what had gone into that mouth, down into that mouth, deep into the recesses of that mouth and disappeared. The circular lip seemed made of scales of steel, and they were washed clean with the water from the race.

On either side of the gigantic mouth was an eye, lidless,

browless, pitiless. They were slightly withdrawn into the head so the Thing could bore into rock without injuring them. Staples tried to estimate their size: all he could do was to avoid their baleful gaze. Then even as he watched, the mouth closed and the head began a semicircular movement, so many degrees to the right, so many degrees to the left and up—and up—and finally the top touched the bottom of the plank Staples was on and then Hrrrrrr—Hrrrrrr and the man knew that it was starting upon the destruction of the second floor. He could not see now as he had been able to see before, but he had an idea that after grinding a while the Thing opened its mouth and swallowed the debris. He looked around the room. Here was where he did his cooking and washing and here was his winter supply of stove wood. A thought came to him.

Working frantically, he pushed the center burner to the middle of the room right over the hole he had cut in the floor. Then he built a fire in it, starting it with a liberal supply of coal oil. He soon had the stove red hot. Opening the door he again filled the stove with oak and then ran for the steps. He was just in time. The floor, cut through, disappeared into the Thing's maw and with it the red-hot stove. Staples yelled in his glee, "A hot pill for you this time, a *hot pill!*"

If the pill did anything, it simply increased the desire of the Thing to destroy, for it kept on till it had bored a hole in this floor equal in size to the holes in the floors below it. Staples saw his food, his furniture, the ancestral relics disappear into the same opening that had consumed the machinery and mill supplies.

On the upper floor the dog howled.

The man slowly went up to the top floor and joined the dog, who had ceased to howl and had begun a low whine. There was a stove on this floor, but there was no food. That did not make any difference to Staples: for some reason he was not hungry anymore: it did not seem to make any difference—nothing seemed to matter or make any difference anymore. Still he had his gun and over fifty cartridges, and he knew that nothing could withstand that.

He lit the lamp and paced the floor in a cold, careless mood. One thing he had determined. He said it over and over to himself.

"This is my home. It has been the home of my family for two hundred years. No devil or beast or worm can make me leave it."

He said it again and again. He felt that if he said it often enough, he would believe it, and if he could only believe it, he might make the Worm believe it. He knew now that it was a Worm, just like the night crawlers he had used so often for bait, only much larger. Yes, that was it. A Worm like a night crawler, only much larger, in fact, very much larger. That made him laugh—to think how much larger this Worm was than the ones he had used for fishing. All through the night he walked the floor and burned the lamp and said, "This is my home. No Worm can make me leave it!" Several times he went down the steps, just a few of them, and shouted the message into the pit as though he wanted the Worm to hear and understand, "This is my home! *No Worm can make me leave it!*"

Morning came. He mounted the ladder that led to the trap door in the roof and opened it. The rain beat in. Still that might be a place of refuge. Crying, he took his Burton and his Rabelais and wrapped them in his raincoat and put them out on the roof, under a box. He took the small pictures of his father and mother and put them with the books. Then in loving kindness he carried the dog up and wrapped him in a woolen blanket. He sat down and waited, and as he did so he recited poetry—anything that came to him, all mixed up, "Come into the garden where there was a man who was so wondrous wise, he jumped into a bramble bush and you're a better man than I am and no one will work for money and the King of Love my Shepherd is,"—and on—and then—

He heard the sliding and the slithering rasping and he knew that the Worm had come again. He waited till the Hrrrrrr—Hrrrrrr told that the wooden floor he was on was being attacked and then he went up the ladder. It was his idea to wait till the Thing had made a large opening, large enough so the eyes could be seen, and then use the fifty bullets—where they would do the most good. So, on the roof, beside the dog, he waited.

He did not have to wait long. First appeared a little hole and then it grew wider and wider till finally the entire floor and the furniture had dropped into the mouth, and the whole opening, thirty feet wide and more than that, was filled with the head, the closed mouth of which came within a few feet of the roof. By the aid of the light from the trap door, Staples could see the eye on the left side. It made a beautiful bull's eye, a magnificent target for his rifle, and he was only a few feet away. He could not miss. Determined to make the most of his last chance to drive his enemy away, he decided to drop down on the creature, walk over to the eye and put the end of the rifle against the eye before he fired. If the first shot worked well, he could retire to the roof and use the other cartridges. He knew that there was some danger—but it was his last hope. After all he knew that when it came to brains he was a man and this Thing was only a Worm. He walked over the head. Surely no sensation could go through such massive scales. He even jumped up and down. Meantime the eye kept looking up at the roof. If it saw the man, it made no signs, gave no evidence. Staples pretended to pull the trigger and then made a running jump for the trap door. It was easy. He did it again, and again. Then he sat on the edge of the door and thought.

He suddenly saw what it all meant. Two hundred years before, his ancestors had started grinding at the mill. For over a hundred and fifty years the mill had been run continuously, often day and night. The vibrations had been transmitted downward through the solid rock. Hundreds of feet below, the Worm had heard them and felt them and thought it was another Worm. It had started to bore in the direction of the noise. It had taken two hundred years to do it, but it had finished the task, it had found the place where its mate should be. For two hundred years it had slowly worked its way through the primitive rock. Why should it worry over a mill and the things within it? Staples saw then that the mill had been but a slight incident in its life. It was probable that it had not even known it was there—the water, the gristmill stones, the red-hot stove, had meant nothing—they had been taken as a part of a day's work. There was only one thing that the Worm was really interested in, but one idea that had reached its consciousness and remained there through two centuries, and that was to find its mate. The eye looked upward.

Staples, at the end, lost courage and decided to fire from a sitting position in the trap door. Taking careful aim, he pulled the trigger. Then he looked carefully to see what damage had resulted. There was none. Either the bullet had gone into the eye and the opening had closed or else it had glanced off. He fired again and again.

Then the mouth opened—wide—wider—until there was nothing under Staples save a yawning void of darkness.

The Worm belched a cloud of black, nauseating vapor. The man, enveloped in the cloud, lost consciousness and fell.

The Mouth closed on him.

On the roof the dog howled.

MIMIC

Donald A. Wollheim

Every day we pass people in the streets without looking at them or noticing them in any real way; they are just "people we don't know." But what if they're more than that? What if some of them are actually creatures *we don't know?*

Donald A. Wollheim is best known as an editor of science fiction, but he has written a number of remarkable stories in the field, and "Mimic" is one of his finest.

It is less than five hundred years since an entire half of the world was discovered. It is less than two hundred years since the discovery of the last continent. The sciences of chemistry and physics go back scarcely one century. The science of aviation goes back forty years. The science of atomics is being born.

And yet we think we know a lot.

We know little or nothing. Some of the most startling things are unknown to us. When they are discovered, they may shock us to the bone.

We search for secrets in the far islands of the Pacific and among the ice fields of the frozen North, while under our very noses, rubbing shoulders with us every day, there may walk the undiscovered. It is a curious fact of nature that that which is in plain view is oft best hidden.

I have always known of the man in the black cloak. Since I

was a child he has always lived on my street, and his eccentricities are so familiar that they go unmentioned except among the casual visitor. Here, in the heart of the largest city in the world, in swarming New York, the eccentric and the odd may flourish unhindered.

As children we had hilarious fun jeering at the man in black when he displayed his fear of women. We watched, in our evil, childish way, for those moments, we tried to get him to show anger. But he ignored us completely and soon we paid him no further heed, even as our parents did.

We saw him only twice a day. Once in the early morning, when we would see his six-foot figure come out of the grimy dark hallway of the tenement at the end of the street and stride down toward the elevated to work—again when he came back at night. He was always dressed in a long, black cloak that came to his ankles, and he wore a wide-brimmed black hat down far over his face. He was a sight from some weird story out of the old lands. But he harmed nobody, and paid attention to nobody.

Nobody—except perhaps women.

When a woman crossed his path, he would stop in his stride and come to a dead halt. We could see that he closed his eyes until she had passed. Then he would snap those wide, watery blue eyes open and march on as if nothing had happened.

He was never known to speak to a woman. He would buy some groceries, maybe once a week, at Antonio's—but only when there were no other patrons there. Antonio said once that he never talked, he just pointed at things he wanted and paid for them in bills that he pulled out of a pocket somewhere under his cloak. Antonio did not like him, but he never had any trouble from him either.

Now that I think of it, nobody ever did have any trouble with him.

We got used to him. We grew up on the street; we saw

him occasionally when he came home and went back into the dark hallway of the house he lived in.

He never had visitors, he never spoke to anyone. And he had once built something in his room out of metal.

He had once, years ago, hauled up some long flat metal sheets, sheets of tin or iron, and they had heard a lot of hammering and banging in his room for several days. But that had stopped and that was all there was to that story.

Where he worked I don't know and never found out. He had money, for he was reputed to pay his rent regularly when the janitor asked for it.

Well, people like that inhabit big cities and nobody knows the story of their lives until they're all over. Or until something strange happens.

I grew up, I went to college, I studied.

Finally I got a job assisting a museum curator. I spent my days mounting beetles and classifying exhibits of stuffed animals and preserved plants, and hundreds and hundreds of insects from all over.

Nature is a strange thing, I learned. You learn that very clearly when you work in a museum. You realize how nature uses the art of camouflage. There are twig insects that look exactly like a leaf or a branch of a tree. Exactly.

Nature is strange and perfect that way. There is a moth in Central America that looks like a wasp. It even has a fake stinger made of hair, which it twists and curls just like a wasp's stinger. It has the same colorings and, even though its body is soft and not armored like a wasp's, it is colored to appear shiny and armored. It even flies in the daytime when wasps do, and not at night like all other moths. It moves like a wasp. It knows somehow that it is helpless and that it can survive only by pretending to be as deadly to other insects as wasps are.

I learned about army ants, and their strange imitators.

Army ants travel in huge columns of thousands and hundreds of thousands. They move along in a flowing stream several yards across and they eat everything in their path. Everything in the jungle is afraid of them. Wasps, bees, snakes, other ants, birds, lizards, beetles—even men run away, or get eaten.

But in the midst of the army ants there also travel many other creatures—creatures that aren't ants at all, and that the army ants would kill if they knew of them. But they don't know of them because these other creatures are disguised. Some of them are beetles that look like ants. They have false markings like ant thoraxes and they run along in imitation of ant speed. There is even one that is so long it is marked like three ants in single file! It moves so fast that the real ants never give it a second glance.

There are weak caterpillars that look like big armored beetles. There are all sorts of things that look like dangerous animals. Animals that are the killers and superior fighters of their groups have no enemies. The army ants and the wasps, the sharks, the hawk, and the felines. So there are a host of weak things that try to hide among them—to mimic them.

And man is the greatest killer, the greatest hunter of them all. The whole world of nature knows man for the irresistible master. The roar of his gun, the cunning of his trap, the strength and agility of his arm place all else beneath him.

Should man then be treated by nature differently from the other dominants, the army ants and the wasps?

It was, as often happens to be the case, sheer luck that I happened to be on the street at the dawning hour when the janitor came running out of the tenement on my street shouting for help. I had been working all night mounting new exhibits.

The policeman on the beat and I were the only people besides the janitor to see the thing that we found in the two dingy rooms occupied by the stranger of the black cloak.

The janitor explained—as the officer and I dashed up the

narrow, rickety stairs—that he had been awakened by the sound of heavy thuds and shrill screams in the stranger's rooms. He had gone out in the hallway to listen.

When we got there, the place was silent. A faint light shone from under the doorway. The policeman knocked, there was no answer. He put his ear to the door and so did I. We heard a faint rustling—a continuous slow rustling as of a breeze blowing paper.

The cop knocked again, but there was still no response.

Then, together, we threw our weight at the door. Two hard blows and the rotten old lock gave way. We burst in.

The room was filthy, the floor covered with scraps of torn paper, bits of detritus and garbage. The room was unfurnished, which I thought was odd.

In the corner there stood a metal box, about four feet square. A tight-box, held together with screws and ropes. It had a lid, opening at the top, which was down and fastened with a sort of wax seal.

The stranger of the black cloak lay in the middle of the floor—dead.

He was still wearing the cloak. The big slouch hat was lying on the floor some distance away. From the inside of the box the faint rustling was coming.

We turned over the stranger, took the cloak off. For several instants we saw nothing amiss and then gradually—horribly— we became aware of some things that were wrong.

His hair was short and curly brown. It stood straight up in its inch-long length. His eyes were open and staring. I noticed first that he had no eyebrows, only a curious dark line in the flesh over each eye.

It was then I realized he had no nose. But no one had ever noticed that before. His skin was oddly mottled. Where the nose should have been there were dark shadowings that made the appearance of a nose, if you only just glanced at him. Like the work of a skillful artist in a painting.

His mouth was as it should be and slightly open—but he had no teeth. His head perched upon a thin neck.

The suit was—not a suit. It was part of him. It was his body.

What we thought was a coat was a huge black wing sheath, like a beetle has. He had a thorax like an insect, only the wing sheath covered it and you couldn't notice it when he wore the cloak. The body bulged out below, tapering off into the two long, thin hind legs. His arms came out from under the top of the "coat." He had a tiny secondary pair of arms folded tightly across his chest. There was a sharp, round hole newly pierced in his chest just above the arms, still oozing a watery liquid.

The janitor fled gibbering. The officer was pale but standing by his duty. I heard him muttering under his breath an endless stream of Hail Marys over and over again.

The lower thorax—the "abdomen"—was very long and insectlike. It was crumpled up now like the wreckage of an airplane fuselage.

I recalled the appearance of a female wasp that had just laid eggs—her thorax had had that empty appearance.

The sight was a shock such as leaves one in full control. The mind rejects it, and it is only in afterthought that one can feel the dim shudder of horror.

The rustling was still coming from the box. I motioned to the white-faced cop and we went over and stood before it. He took the nightstick and knocked away the waxen seal.

Then we heaved and pulled the lid open.

A wave of noxious vapor assailed us. We staggered back as suddenly a stream of flying things shot out of the huge iron container. The window was open, and straight out into the first glow of dawn they flew.

There must have been dozens of them. They were about two or three inches long and they flew on wide gauzy beetle wings. They looked like little men, strangely terrifying as they flew—clad in their black suits, with their expressionless faces and their dots of watery blue eyes. And they flew out on transparent wings that came from under their black beetle coats.

I ran to the window, fascinated, almost hypnotized. The horror of it had not reached my mind at once. Afterward I have had spasms of numbing terror as my mind tries to put the things together. The whole business was so utterly unexpected.

We knew of army ants and their imitators, yet it never occurred to us that we too were army ants of a sort. We knew of stick insects and it never occurred to us that there might be others that disguise themselves to fool, not other animals, but the supreme animal himself—man.

We found some bones in the bottom of that iron case afterwards. But we couldn't identify them. Perhaps we did not try very hard. They might have been human. . . .

I suppose the stranger of the black cloak did not fear women so much as it distrusted them. Women notice men, perhaps, more closely than other men do. Women might become suspicious sooner of the inhumanity, the deception. And then there might perhaps have been some touch of instinctive feminine jealousy. The stranger was disguised as a man, but its sex was surely female. The things in the box were its young.

But it is the other thing I saw when I ran to the window that has shaken me the most. The policeman did not see it. Nobody else saw it but me, and I only for an instant.

Nature practices deceptions in every angle. Evolution will create a being for any niche that can be found, no matter how unlikely.

When I went to the window, I saw the small cloud of flying things rising up into the sky and sailing away into the purple distance. The dawn was breaking and the first rays of the sun were just striking over the housetops.

Shaken, I looked away from that fourth-floor tenement room over the roofs of lower buildings. Chimneys and walls and empty clotheslines made the scenery over which the tiny mass of horror passed.

And then I saw a chimney, not thirty feet away on the next roof. It was squat and of red brick and had two black pipe ends flush with its top. I saw it suddenly vibrate, oddly. And I saw its red brick surface seem to peel away, and the black pipe openings turn suddenly white.

I saw two big eyes staring into the sky.

A great, flat-winged thing detached itself silently from the surface of the real chimney and darted after the cloud of flying things.

I watched until all had lost themselves in the sky.

IT

Theodore Sturgeon

All life is a process of change, and the wonders of creation continue to proliferate as new forms of life come into being. Usually these new life-forms are minor mutations from the norm, genetic accidents—but might there not also be other ways in which a new creature could come to life? Something immensely powerful, and curious about what's inside other living creatures. . . .

Theodore Sturgeon is one of the finest writers of science fiction and fantasy; he is the author of the classic novel More Than Human *and many, many more.*

It walked in the woods.

It was never born. It existed. Under the pine needles the fires burn, deep and smokeless in the mold. In heat and in darkness and decay there is growth. There is life and there is growth. It grew, but it was not alive. It walked unbreathing through the woods, and thought and saw and was hideous and strong, and it was not born and it did not live. It grew and moved about without living.

It crawled out of the darkness and hot, damp mold into the cool of a morning. It was huge. It was lumped and crusted with its own hateful substances, and pieces of it dropped off as it went its way, dropped off and lay writhing, and stilled, and sank putrescent into the forest loam.

It had no mercy, no laughter, no beauty. It had strength and great intelligence. And—perhaps it could not be destroyed. It crawled out of its mound in the wood and lay pulsing in the sunlight for a long moment. Patches of it shone wetly in the golden glow, parts of it were nubbled and flaked. And whose dead bones had given it the form of a man?

It scrabbled painfully with its half-formed hands, beating the ground and the bole of a tree. It rolled and lifted itself up on its crumbling elbows, and it tore up a great handful of herbs and shredded them against its chest, and it paused and gazed at the gray-green juices with intelligent calm. It wavered to its feet, and seized a young sapling and destroyed it, folding the slender trunk back on itself again and again, watching attentively the useless, fibered splinters. And it snatched up a fear-frozen field creature, crushing it slowly, letting blood and pulpy flesh and fur ooze from between its fingers, run down and rot on the forearms.

It began searching.

Kimbo drifted through the tall grasses like a puff of dust, his bushy tail curled tightly over his back and his long jaws agape. He ran with an easy lope, loving his freedom and the power of his flanks and furry shoulders. His tongue lolled listlessly over his lips. His lips were black and serrated, and each tiny pointed liplet swayed with his doggy gallop. Kimbo was all dog, all healthy animal.

He leaped high over a boulder and landed with a startled yelp as a long-eared coney shot from its hiding place under the rock. Kimbo hurtled after it, grunting with each great thrust of his legs. The rabbit bounced just ahead of him, keeping its distance, its ears flattened on its curving back and its little legs nibbling away at distance hungrily. It stopped, and Kimbo pounced, and the rabbit shot away at a tangent and popped into a hollow log. Kimbo yelped again and rushed snuffling at the log, and knowing his failure, curvetted

but once around the stump and ran on into the forest. The
thing that watched from the wood raised its crusted arms and
waited for Kimbo.

Kimbo sensed it there, standing dead still by the path. To
him it was a bulk that smelled of carrion not fit to roll in, and
he snuffled distastefully and ran to pass it.

The thing let him come abreast and dropped a heavy
twisted fist on him. Kimbo saw it coming and curled up tight
as he ran, and the hand clipped stunningly on his rump,
sending him rolling and yipping down the slope. Kimbo strad-
dled to his feet, shook his head, shook his body with a deep
growl, came back to the silent thing with green murder in his
eyes. He walked stiffly, straight-legged, his tail as low as his
lowered head and a ruff of fury around his neck. The thing
raised its arms again, waited.

Kimbo slowed, then flipped himself through the air at the
monster's throat. His jaws closed on it; his teeth clicked together through a mass of filth, and he fell choking and
snarling at its feet. The thing leaned down and struck twice,
and after the dog's back was broken, it sat beside him and
began to tear him apart.

"Be back in an hour or so," said Alton Drew, picking up
his rifle from the corner behind the woodbox. His brother
laughed.

"Old Kimbo 'bout runs your life, Alton," he said.

"Ah, I know the ol' devil," said Alton. "When I whistle for
him for half an hour and he don't show up, he's in a jam or
he's treed something wuth shootin' at. The ol' son of a gun
calls me by not answerin'."

Cory Drew shoved a full glass of milk over to his nine-year-
old daughter and smiled. "You think as much o' that houn'
dog o' yours as I do of Babe here."

Babe slid off her chair and ran to her uncle. "Gonna catch
me the bad fella, Uncle Alton?" she shrilled. The "bad fella"

was Cory's invention—the one who lurked in corners ready to pounce on little girls who chased the chickens and played around mowing machines and hurled green apples with a powerful young arm at the sides of the hogs, to hear the synchronized thud and grunt; little girls who swore with an Austrian accent like an ex-hired man they had had; who dug caves in haystacks till they tipped over, and kept pet crawfish in tomorrow's milk cans, and rode work horses to a lather in the night pasture.

"Get back here and keep away from Uncle Alton's gun!" said Cory. "If you see the bad fella, Alton, chase him back here. He has a date with Babe here for that stunt of hers last night." The preceding evening, Babe had kind-heartedly poured pepper on the cows' salt block.

"Don't worry, kiddo," grinned her uncle, "I'll bring you the bad fella's hide if he don't get me first."

Alton Drew walked up the path toward the wood, thinking about Babe. She was a phenomenon—a pampered farm child. Ah, well—she had to be. They'd both loved Clissa Drew, and she'd married Cory, and they had to love Clissa's child. Funny thing, love. Alton was a man's man, and thought things out that way; and his reaction to love was a strong and frightened one. He knew what love was because he felt it still for his brother's wife and would feel it as long as he lived for Babe. It led him through his life, and yet he embarrassed himself by thinking of it. Loving a dog was an easy thing, because you and the old devil could love one another completely without talking about it. The smell of gun smoke and wet fur in the rain were perfume enough for Alton Drew, a grunt of satisfaction and the scream of something hunted and hit were poetry enough. They weren't like love for a human that choked his throat so he could not say words he could not have thought of anyway. So Alton loved his dog Kimbo and his Winchester for all to see, and let his love for his brother's women, Clissa and Babe, eat at him quietly and unmentioned.

His quick eyes saw the fresh indentations in the soft earth behind the boulder, which showed where Kimbo had turned and leaped with a single surge, chasing the rabbit. Ignoring the tracks, he looked for the nearest place where a rabbit might hide, and strolled over to the stump. Kimbo had been there, he saw, and had been there too late. "You're an ol' fool," muttered Alton, "y'can't catch a coney by chasin' it. You want to cross him up someway." He gave a peculiar trilling whistle, sure that Kimbo was digging frantically under some nearby stump for a rabbit that was three counties away by now. No answer. A little puzzled, Alton went back to the path. "He never done this before," he said softly.

He cocked his .32-40 and cradled it. At the county fair someone had once said of Alton Drew that he could shoot at a handful of corn and peas thrown in the air and hit only the corn. Once he split a bullet on the blade of a knife and put two candles out. He had no need to fear anything that could be shot at. That's what he believed.

The thing in the woods looked curiously down at what it had done to Kimbo, and tried to moan the way Kimbo had before he died. It stood a minute storing away facts in its foul, unemotional mind. Blood was warm. The sunlight was warm. Things that moved and bore fur had a muscle to force the thick liquid through tiny tubes in their bodies. The liquid coagulated after a time. The liquid on rooted green things was thinner and the loss of a limb did not mean loss of life. It was very interesting, but the thing, the mold with a mind, was not pleased. Neither was it displeased. Its accidental urge was a thirst for knowledge, and it was only—interested.

It was growing late, and the sun reddened and rested a while on the hilly horizon, teaching the clouds to be inverted flames. The thing threw up its head suddenly, noticing the dusk. Night was ever a strange thing, even for those of us who have known it in life. It would have been frightening for the monster had it been capable of fright, but it could only be curious; it could only reason from what it had observed.

What was happening? It was getting harder to see. Why? It threw its shapeless head from side to side. It was true—things were dim, and growing dimmer. Things were changing shape, taking on a new and darker color. What did the creatures it had crushed and torn apart see? How did they see? The larger one, the one that had attacked, had used two organs in its head. That must have been it, because after the thing had torn off two of the dog's legs it had struck at the hairy muzzle; and the dog, seeing the blow coming, had dropped folds of skin over the organs—closed its eyes. Ergo, the dog saw with its eyes. But then after the dog was dead, and its body still, repeated blows had had no effect on the eyes. They remained open and staring. The logical conclusion was, then, that a being that had ceased to live and breathe and move about lost the use of its eyes. It must be that to lose sight was, conversely, to die. Dead things did not walk about. They lay down and did not move. Therefore the thing in the wood concluded that it must be dead, and so it lay down by the path, not far away from Kimbo's scattered body, lay down and believed itself dead.

Alton Drew came up through the dusk to the wood. He was frankly worried. He whistled again, and then called, and there was still no response, and he said again, "The ol' flea-bus never done this before," and shook his heavy head. It was past milking time, and Cory would need him. "Kimbo!" he roared. The cry echoed through the shadows, and Alton flipped on the safety catch of his rifle and put the butt on the ground beside the path. Leaning on it, he took off his cap and scratched the back of his head, wondering. The rifle butt sank into what he thought was soft earth; he staggered and stepped into the chest of the thing that lay beside the path. His foot went up to the ankle in its yielding rottenness, and he swore and jumped back.

"*Whew!* Somp'n sure dead as hell there! Ugh!" He swabbed at his boot with a handful of leaves while the monster lay in the growing blackness with the edges of the deep footprint in its chest sliding into it, filling it up. It lay there regarding him dimly out of its muddy eyes, thinking it was dead because of the darkness, watching the articulation of Alton Drew's joints, wondering at this new uncautious creature.

Alton cleaned the butt of his gun with more leaves and went on up the path, whistling anxiously for Kimbo.

Clissa Drew stood in the door of the milkshed, very lovely in red-checked gingham and a blue apron. Her hair was clean yellow, parted in the middle and stretched tautly back to a heavy braided knot. "Cory! Alton!" she called a little sharply.

"Well?" Cory responded gruffly from the barn, where he was stripping off the Ayrshire. The dwindling streams of milk plopped pleasantly into the froth of a full pail.

"I've called and called," said Clissa. "Supper's cold, and Babe won't eat until you come. Why—where's Alton?"

Cory grunted, heaved the stool out of the way, threw over the stanchion lock and slapped the Ayrshire on the rump. The cow backed and filled like a towboat, clattered down the line and out into the barnyard. "Ain't back yet."

"Not back?" Clissa came in and stood beside him as he sat by the next cow, put his forehead against the warm flank. "But, Cory, he said he'd—"

"Yeh, yeh, I know. He said he'd be back fer the milkin'. I heard him. Well, he ain't."

"And you have to—oh, Cory, I'll help you finish up. Alton would be back if he could. Maybe he's—"

"Maybe he's treed a blue jay," snapped her husband. "Him

an' that damn dog." He gestured hugely with one hand while the other went on milking. "I got twenty-six head o' cows to milk. I got pigs to feed an' chickens to put to bed. I got to toss hay for the mare and turn the team out. I got harness to mend and a wire down in the night pasture. I got wood to split an' carry." He milked for a moment in silence, chewing on his lip. Clissa stood twisting her hands together, trying to think of something to stem the tide. It wasn't the first time Alton's hunting had interfered with the chores. "So I got to go ahead with it. I can't interfere with Alton's spoorin'. Every damn time that hound o' his smells out a squirrel I go without my supper. I'm gettin' sick and—"

"Oh, I'll help you!" said Clissa. She was thinking of the spring, when Kimbo had held four hundred pounds of raging black bear at bay until Alton could put a bullet in its brain, the time Babe had found a bearcub and started to carry it home, and had fallen into a freshet, cutting her head. You can't hate a dog that has saved your child for you, she thought.

"You'll do nothin' of the kind!" Cory growled. "Get back to the house. You'll find work enough there. I'll be along when I can. Dammit, Clissa, don't cry! I didn't mean to— Oh, shucks!" He got up and put his arms around her. "I'm wrought up," he said. "Go on now. I'd no call to speak that way to you. I'm sorry. Go back to Babe. I'll put a stop to this for good tonight. I've had enough. There's work here for four farmers, an' all we've got is me an' that . . . that huntsman.

"Go on now, Clissa."

"All right," she said into his shoulder. "But, Cory, hear him out first when he comes back. He might be unable to come back. He might be unable to come back this time. Maybe he . . . he—"

"Ain't nothin' kin hurt my brother that a bullet will hit. He can take care of himself. He's got no excuse good enough this time. Go on, now. Make the kid eat."

Clissa went back to the house, her young face furrowed. If Cory quarreled with Alton now and drove him away, what with the drought and the creamery about to close and all, they just couldn't manage. Hiring a man was out of the question. Cory'd have to work himself to death, and he just wouldn't be able to make it. No one man could. She sighed and went into the house. It was seven o'clock, and the milking not done yet. Oh, why did Alton have to—

Babe was in bed at nine when Clissa heard Cory in the shed, slinging the wire cutters into a corner. "Alton back yet?" they both said at once as Cory stepped into the kitchen; and as she shook her head he clumped over to the stove, and lifting a lid, spat into the coals. "Come to bed," he said.

She laid down her stitching and looked at his broad back. He was twenty-eight, and he walked and acted like a man ten years older, and looked like a man five years younger. "I'll be up in a while," Clissa said.

Cory glanced at the corner behind the woodbox where Alton's rifle usually stood, then made an unspellable, disgusted sound and sat down to take off his heavy muddy shoes.

"It's after nine," Clissa volunteered timidly. Cory said nothing, reaching for his house slippers.

"Cory, you're not going to—"

"Not going to what?"

"Oh, nothing. I just thought that maybe Alton—"

"Alton," Cory flared. "The dog goes hunting field mice. Alton goes hunting the dog. Now you want me to go hunting Alton. That's what you want?"

"I just— He was never this late before."

"I won't do it! Go out lookin' for him at nine o'clock in the night? I'll be damned! He has no call to use us so, Clissa."

Clissa said nothing. She went to the stove, peered into the wash boiler, set aside at the back of the range. When she turned around, Cory had his shoes and coat on again.

"I knew you'd go," she said. Her voice smiled though she did not.

"I'll be back durned soon," said Cory. "I don't reckon he's strayed far. It is late. I ain't feared for him, but—" He broke his 12-gauge shotgun, looked through the barrels, slipped two shells in the breech and a box of them into his pocket. "Don't wait up," he said over his shoulder as he went out.

"I won't," Clissa replied to the closed door, and went back to her stitching by the lamp.

The path up the slope to the wood was very dark when Cory went up it, peering and calling. The air was chill and quiet, and a fetid odor of mold hung in it. Cory blew the taste of it out through impatient nostrils, drew it in again with the next breath, and swore. "Nonsense," he muttered. "Houn' dawg. Huntin', at ten in th' night, too. Alton!" he bellowed. "Alton Drew!" Echoes answered him, and he entered the wood. The huddled thing he passed in the dark heard him and felt the vibrations of his footsteps and did not move because it thought it was dead.

Cory strode on, looking around and ahead and not down since his feet knew the path.

"Alton!"

"That you, Cory?"

Cory Drew froze. That corner of the wood was thickly set and as dark as a burial vault. The voice he heard was choked, quiet, penetrating.

"Alton?"

"I found Kimbo, Cory."

"Where the hell have you been?" shouted Cory furiously. He disliked this pitch-darkness; he was afraid at the tense hopelessness of Alton's voice, and he mistrusted his ability to stay angry at his brother.

"I called him, Cory. I whistled at him, an' the ol' devil didn't answer."

"I can say the same for you, you . . . you louse. Why

weren't you to milkin'? Where are you? You caught in a trap?"

"The houn' never missed answerin' me before, you know," said the tight, monotonous voice from the darkness.

"Alton! What the devil's the matter with you? What do I care if your mutt didn't answer? Where—"

"I guess because he ain't never died before," said Alton, refusing to be interrupted.

"You *what!*" Cory clicked his lips together twice and then said, "Alton, you turned crazy? What's that you say?"

"Kimbo's dead."

"Kim—— Oh! Oh!" Cory was seeing that picture again in his mind—Babe sprawled unconscious in the freshet, and Kimbo raging and snapping against a monster bear, holding her back until Alton could get there. "What happened, Alton?" he asked more quietly.

"I aim to find out. Someone tore him up."

"*Tore him up?*"

"There ain't a bit of him left tacked together, Cory. Every damn joint in his body tore apart. Guts out of him."

"Good God! Bear, you reckon?"

"No bear, nor nothin' on four legs. He's all here. None of him's been et. Whoever done it just killed him an'—tore him up."

"Good God!" Cory said again. "Who could've—" There was a long silence, then. "Come 'long home," he said almost gently. "There's no call for you to set up by him all night."

"I'll set. I aim to be here at sunup, an' I'm going to start trackin', an' I'm goin' to keep trackin' till I find the one done this job on Kimbo."

"You're drunk or crazy, Alton."

"I ain't drunk. You can think what you like about the rest of it. I'm stickin' here."

"We got a farm back yonder. Remember? I ain't going to

milk twenty-six head o' cows again in the mornin' like I did jest now, Alton."

"Somebody's got to. I can't be there. I guess you'll just have to, Cory."

"You dirty scum!" Cory screamed. "You'll come back with me now or I'll know why!"

Alton's voice was still tight, half sleepy. "Don't you come no nearer, bud."

Cory kept moving toward Alton's voice.

"I said"—the voice was very quiet now—"*stop where you are.*" Cory kept coming. A sharp click told of the release of the .32-40's safety. Cory stopped.

"You got your gun on me, Alton?" Cory whispered.

"Thass right, bud. You ain't a-trompin' up these tracks for me. I need 'em at sunup."

A full minute passed, and the only sound in the blackness was that of Cory's pained breathing. Finally:

"I got my gun, too, Alton. Come home."

"You can't see to shoot me."

"We're even on that."

"We ain't. I know just where you stand, Cory. I been here four hours."

"My gun scatters."

"My gun kills."

Without another word, Cory Drew turned on his heel and stamped back to the farm.

Black and liquidescent it lay in the blackness, not alive, not understanding death, believing itself dead. Things that were alive saw and moved about. Things that were not alive could do neither. It rested its muddy gaze on the line of trees at the crest of the rise, and deep within it thoughts trickled wetly. It lay huddled, dividing its new-found facts, dissecting them as it had dissected live things when there was light, comparing, concluding, pigeonholing.

The trees at the top of the slope could just be seen, as their trunks were a fraction of a shade lighter than the dark sky behind them. At length they, too, disappeared, and for a moment sky and trees were a monotone. The thing knew it was dead now, and like many a being before it, it wondered how long it must stay like this. And then the sky beyond the trees grew a little lighter. That was a manifestly impossible occurrence, thought the thing, but it could see it and it must be so. Did dead things live again? That was curious. What about dismembered dead things? It would wait and see.

The sun came hand over hand up a beam of light. A bird somewhere made a high yawning peep, and as an owl killed a shrew, a skunk pounced on another, so that the night-shift deaths and those of the day could go on without cessation. Two flowers nodded archly to each other, comparing their pretty clothes. A dragonfly nymph decided it was tired of looking serious and cracked its back open, to crawl out and dry gauzily. The first golden ray sheared down between the trees, through the grasses, passed over the mass in the shadowed bushes. "I am alive again," thought the thing that could not possibly live. "I am alive, for I see clearly." It stood up on its thick legs, up into the golden glow. In a little while the wet flakes that had grown during the night dried in the sun, and when it took its first steps, they cracked off and a small shower of them fell away. It walked up the slope to find Kimbo, to see if he, too, was alive again.

Babe let the sun come into her room by opening her eyes. Uncle Alton was gone—that was the first thing that ran through her head. Dad had come home last night and had shouted at mother for an hour. Alton was plumb crazy. He'd turned a gun on his own brother. If Alton ever came ten feet into Cory's land, Cory would fill him so full of holes, he'd look like a tumbleweed. Alton was lazy, shiftless, selfish, and one or two other things of questionable taste but undoubted vividness. Babe knew her father. Uncle Alton would never be safe in this county.

She bounced out of bed in the enviable way of the very young, and ran to the window. Cory was trudging down to the night pasture with two bridles over his arm, to get the team. There were kitchen noises from downstairs.

Babe ducked her head in the washbowl and shook off the water like a terrier before she toweled. Trailing clean shirt and dungarees, she went to the head of the stairs, slid into the shirt, and began her morning ritual with the trousers. One step down was a step through the right leg. One more, and she was into the left. Then, bouncing step by step on both feet, buttoning one button per step, she reached the bottom fully dressed and ran into the kitchen.

"Didn't Uncle Alton come back a-tall, Mum?"

"Morning, Babe. No, dear." Clissa was too quiet, smiling too much, Babe thought shrewdly. Wasn't happy.

"Where'd he go, Mum?"

"We don't know, Babe. Sit down and eat your breakfast."

"What's a misbegotten, Mum?" the Babe asked suddenly. Her mother nearly dropped the dish she was drying. "Babe! You must never say that again!"

"Oh. Well, why is Uncle Alton, then?"

"Why is he what?"

Babe's mouth muscled around an outsize spoonful of oatmeal. "A misbe——"

"Babe!"

"All right, Mum," said Babe with her mouth full. "Well, why?"

"I told Cory not to shout last night," Clissa said half to herself.

"Well, whatever it means, he isn't," said Babe with finality. "Did he go hunting again?"

"He went to look for Kimbo, darling."

"Kimbo? Oh Mummy, is Kimbo gone, too? Didn't he come back either?"

"No, dear. Oh, please, Babe, stop asking questions!"

"All right. Where do you think they went?"

"Into the north woods. Be quiet."

Babe gulped away at her breakfast. An idea struck her; and as she thought of it she ate slower and slower and cast more and more glances at her mother from under the lashes of her tilted eyes. It would be awful if Daddy did anything to Uncle Alton. Someone ought to warn him.

Babe was halfway to the wood when Alton's .32-40 sent echoes giggling up and down the valley.

Cory was in the south thirty, riding a cultivator and cussing at the team of grays when he heard the gun. "Hoa," he called to the horses, and sat a moment to listen to the sound. "One-two-three. Four," he counted. "Saw someone, blasted away at him. Had a chance to take aim and give him another, careful. My God!" He threw up the cultivator points and steered the team into the shade of three oaks. He hobbled the gelding with swift tosses of a spare strap and headed for the woods. "Alton a killer," he murmured, and doubled back to the house for his gun. Clissa was standing just outside the door.

"Get shells!" he snapped and flung into the house. Clissa followed him. He was strapping his hunting knife on before she could get a box off the shelf. "Cory—"

"Hear that gun, did you? Alton's off his nut. He don't waste lead. He shot at someone just then, and he wasn't fixin' to shoot pa'tridges when I saw him last. He was out to get a man. Gimme my gun."

"Cory, Babe—"

"You keep her here. Oh, God, this is a helluva mess. I can't stand much more." Cory ran out the door.

Clissa caught his arm: "Cory, I'm trying to tell you. Babe isn't here. I've called, and she isn't here."

Cory's heavy, young-old face tautened. "Babe— Where did you last see her?"

"Breakfast." Clissa was crying now.

"She say where she was going?"

"No. She asked a lot of questions about Alton and where he'd gone."

"Did you say?"

Clissa's eyes widened, and she nodded, biting the back of her hand.

"You shouldn't ha' done that, Clissa," he gritted, and ran toward the woods, Clissa looking after him, and in that moment she could have killed herself.

Cory ran with his head up, straining with his legs and lungs and eyes at the long path. He puffed up the slope to the wood, agonized for breath after the forty-five minutes' heavy going. He couldn't even notice the damp smell of mold in the air.

He caught a movement in a thicket to his right, and dropped. Struggling to keep his breath, he crept forward until he could see clearly. There was something in there, all right. Something black, keeping still. Cory relaxed his legs and torso completely to make it easier for his heart to pump some strength back into them, and slowly raised the 12-gauge until it bore on the thing hidden in the thicket.

"Come out!" Cory said when he could speak.

Nothing happened.

"Come out or by God I'll shoot!" rasped Cory.

There was a long moment of silence, and his finger tightened on the trigger.

"You asked for it," he said, and as he fired, the thing leaped sideways into the open, screaming.

It was a thin little man dressed in sepulchral black and bearing the rosiest baby face Cory had ever seen. The face was twisted with fright and pain. The man scrambled to his feet and hopped up and down saying over and over, "Oh, my hand. Don't shoot again! Oh, my hand. Don't shoot again!" He stopped after a bit, when Cory had climbed to his feet, and he regarded the farmer out of sad china-blue eyes. "You shot me," he said reproachfully, holding up a little bloody hand. "Oh, my goodness."

Cory said, "Now, who the hell are you?"

The man immediately became hysterical, mouthing such a flood of broken sentences that Cory stepped back a pace and half raised his gun in self-defense. It seemed to consist mostly of "I lost my papers," and "I didn't do it," and "It was horrible, horrible, horrible," and "The dead man," and "Oh, don't shoot again."

Cory tried twice to ask him a question, and then he stepped over and knocked the man down. He lay on the ground writhing and moaning and blubbering and putting his bloody hand to his mouth where Cory had hit him.

"Now what's going on around here?"

The man rolled over and sat up. "I didn't do it!" he sobbed. "I didn't. I was walking along and I heard the gun and I heard some swearing and an awful scream and I went over there and peeped and I saw the dead man and I ran away and you came and I hid and you shot me and—"

"*Shut up!*" The man did, as if a switch had been thrown. "Now," said Cory, pointing along the path, "you say there's a dead man up there?"

The man nodded and began crying in earnest. Cory helped him up. "Follow this path back to my farmhouse," he said. "Tell my wife to fix up your hand. *Don't* tell her anything else. And wait there until I come. Hear?"

"Yes. Thank you. Oh, thank you. *Snff.*"

"Go on now." Cory gave him a gentle shove in the right direction and went alone, in cold fear, up the path to the spot where he had found Alton the night before.

He found him here now, too, and Kimbo. Kimbo and Alton had spent several years together in the deepest friendship; they had hunted and fought and slept together, and the lives they owed each other were finished now. They were dead together.

It was terrible that they died the same way. Cory Drew was a strong man, but he gasped and fainted dead away when he saw what the thing of the mold had done to his brother and his brother's dog.

The little man in black hurried down the path, whimpering and holding his injured hand as if he rather wished he could limp with it. After a while the whimper faded away, and the hurried stride changed to a walk as the gibbering terror of the last hour receded. He drew two deep breaths, said: "My goodness!" and felt almost normal. He bound a linen handkerchief around his wrist, but the hand kept bleeding. He tried the elbow, and that made it hurt. So he stuffed the handkerchief back in his pocket and simply waved the hand stupidly in the air until the blood clotted. He did not see the great moist horror that clumped along behind him, although his nostrils crinkled with its foulness.

The monster had three holes close together on its chest, and one hole in the middle of its slimy forehead. It had three close-set pits in its back and one on the back of its head. These marks were where Alton Drew's bullets had struck and passed through. Half of the monster's face was sloughed away, and there was a deep indentation on its shoulder. This was what Alton Drew's gun butt had done after he clubbed it and struck at the thing that would not lie down after he put his four bullets through it. When these things happened the monster was not hurt or angry. It only wondered why Alton Drew acted that way. Now it followed the little man without hurrying at all, matching his stride step by step and dropping little particles of muck behind it.

The little man went on out of the wood and stood with his back against a big tree at the forest's edge, and he thought. Enough had happened to him here. What good would it do to stay and face a horrible murder inquest, just to continue this silly, vague search? There was supposed to be the ruin of an old, old hunting lodge deep in this wood somewhere, and perhaps it would hold the evidence he wanted. But it was a vague report—vague enough to be forgotten without regret. It would be the height of foolishness to stay for all the hicktown red tape that would follow that ghastly affair back in the woods. Ergo, it would be ridiculous to follow that farmer's advice, to go to his house and wait for him. He would go back to town.

The monster was leaning against the other side of the big tree.

The little man snuffled disgustedly at a sudden overpowering odor of rot. He reached for his handkerchief, fumbled and dropped it. As he bent to pick it up, the monster's arm *whuffed* heavily in the air where his head had been—a blow that would certainly have removed that baby-face protuberance. The man stood up and would have put the handkerchief to his nose had it not been so bloody. The creature behind the tree lifted its arm again just as the little man tossed the handkerchief away and stepped out into the field, heading across country to the distant highway that would take him back to town. The monster pounced on the handkerchief, picked it up, studied it, tore it across several times and inspected the tattered edges. Then it gazed vacantly at the disappearing figure of the little man, and finding him no longer interesting, turned back into the woods.

Babe broke into a trot at the sound of the shots. It was important to warn Uncle Alton about what her father had said, but it was more interesting to find out what he had bagged. Oh, he'd bagged it, all right. Uncle Alton never fired without killing. This was about the first time she had ever heard him blast away like that. Must be a bear, she thought excitedly, tripping over a root, sprawling, rolling to her feet again, without noticing the tumble. She'd love to have another bearskin in her room. Where would she put it? Maybe they could line it and she could have it for a blanket. Uncle Alton could sit on it and read to her in the evening—Oh, no. No. Not with this trouble between him and dad. Oh, if she could only do something! She tried to run faster, worried and anticipating, but she was out of breath and went more slowly instead.

At the top of the rise by the edge of the woods she stopped and looked back. Far down in the valley lay the south thirty. She scanned it carefully, looking for her father. The new furrows and the old were sharply defined, and her keen eyes saw immediately that Cory had left the line with the cultivator and had angled the team over to the shade trees without finishing his row. That wasn't like him. She could see the team now, and Cory's pale-blue denim was nowhere in sight. She giggled lightly to herself as she thought of the way she would fool her father. And the little sound of laughter drowned out, for her, the sound of Alton's hoarse dying scream.

She reached and crossed the path and slid through the brush beside it. The shots came from up around here somewhere. She stopped and listened several times, and then suddenly heard something coming toward her, fast. She ducked under cover, terrified, and a little baby-faced man in black, his blue eyes wide with horror, crashed blindly past her, the leather case he carried catching on the branches. It spun a moment and then fell right in front of her. The man never missed it.

Babe lay there for a long moment and then picked up the case and faded into the woods. Things were happening too fast for her. She wanted Uncle Alton, but she dared not call. She stopped again and strained her ears. Back toward the

edge of the woods she heard her father's voice, and another's
—probably the man who had dropped the briefcase. She dared
not go over there. Filled with enjoyable terror, she thought
hard, then snapped her fingers in triumph. She and Alton
had played Injun many times up here; they had a whole repertoire of secret signals. She had practiced birdcalls until she
knew them better than the birds themselves. What would it
be? Ah—bluejay. She threw back her head and by some youth-
ful alchemy produced a nerve-shattering screech that would
have done justice to any jay that ever flew. She repeated it,
and then twice more.

The response was immediate—the call of a bluejay, four
times, spaced two and two. Babe nodded to herself happily.
That was the signal that they were to meet immediately at
The Place. The Place was a hideout that he had discovered
and shared with her, and not another soul knew of it; an
angle of rock beside a stream not far away. It wasn't exactly a
cave, but almost. Enough so to be entrancing. Babe trotted
happily away toward the brook. She had just known that
Uncle Alton would remember the call of the bluejay, and
what it meant.

In the tree that arched over Alton's scattered body perched
a large jaybird, preening itself and shining in the sun. Quite
unconscious of the presence of death, hardly noticing the
Babe's realistic cry, it screamed again four times, two and two.

It took Cory more than a moment to recover himself from
what he had seen. He turned away from it and leaned weakly
against a pine, panting. Alton. That was Alton lying there, in
—parts.

"God! God, God, God—"

Gradually his strength returned, and he forced himself to
turn again. Stepping carefully, he bent and picked up the
.32-40. Its barrel was bright and clean, but the butt and stock

were smeared with some kind of stinking rottenness. Where had he seen the stuff before? Somewhere—no matter. He cleaned it off absently, throwing the befouled bandanna away afterward. Through his mind ran Alton's words—was that only last night?—"*I'm goin' to start trackin', an' I'm goin' to keep trackin' till I find the one done this job on Kimbo.*"

Cory searched shrinkingly until he found Alton's box of shells. The box was wet and sticky. That made it—better, somehow. A bullet wet with Alton's blood was the right thing to use. He went away a short distance, circled around till he found heavy footprints, then came back.

"I'm a-trackin' for you, bud," he whispered thickly, and began. Through the brush he followed its wavering spoor, amazed at the amount of filthy mold about, gradually associating it with the thing that had killed his brother. There was nothing in the world for him anymore but hate and doggedness. Cursing himself for not getting Alton home last night, he followed the tracks to the edge of the woods. They led him to a big tree there, and there he saw something else— the footprints of the little city man. Nearby lay some tattered scraps of linen, and—what was that?

Another set of prints—small ones. Small, stub-toed ones.

"Babe!"

No answer. The wind sighed. Somewhere a bluejay called.

Babe stopped and turned when she heard her father's voice, faint with distance, piercing.

"Listen at him holler," she crooned delightedly. "Gee, he sounds mad." She sent a jaybird's call disrespectfully back to him and hurried to The Place.

It consisted of a mammoth boulder beside the brook. Some upheaval in the glacial age had cleft it, cutting out a huge V-shaped chunk. The widest part of the cleft was at the water's edge, and the narrowest was hidden by bushes. It made a little ceilingless room, rough and uneven and full of potholes and cavelets inside, and yet with quite a level floor. The open end was at the water's edge.

Babe parted the bushes and peered down the cleft.

"Uncle Alton!" she called softly. There was no answer. Oh, well, he'd be along. She scrambled in and slid down to the floor.

She loved it here. It was shaded and cool, and the chattering stream filled it with shifting golden lights and laughing gurgles. She called again, on principle, and then perched on an outcropping to wait. It was only then she realized that she still carried the little man's briefcase.

She turned it over a couple of times and then opened it. It was divided in the middle by a leather wall. On one side were a few papers in a large yellow envelope, and on the other some sandwiches, a candy bar, and an apple. With a youngster's complacent acceptance of manna from heaven, Babe fell to. She saved one sandwich for Alton, mainly because she didn't like its highly spiced bologna. The rest made quite a feast.

She was a little worried when Alton hadn't arrived, even after she had consumed the apple core. She got up and tried to skim some flat pebbles across the rolling brook, and she stood on her hands, and she tried to think of a story to tell herself, and she tried just waiting. Finally, in desperation, she turned again to the briefcase, took out the papers, curled up by the rocky wall and began to read them. It was something to do, anyway.

There was an old newspaper clipping that told about strange wills that people had left. An old lady had once left a lot of money to whoever would make the trip from the Earth to the Moon and back. Another had financed a home for cats whose masters and mistresses had died. A man left thousands of dollars to the first person who could solve a certain mathematical problem and prove his solution. But one item was blue-penciled. It was:

One of the strangest of wills still in force is that of Thaddeus M. Kirk, who died in 1920. It appears that he built an elaborate mausoleum with burial vaults for all the remains of his family. He collected and removed caskets from all over the country to fill the designated niches. Kirk was the last of his line; there were no relatives when he died. His will stated that the mausoleum was to be kept in repair permanently, and that a certain sum was to be set aside as a reward for whoever could produce the body of his grandfather, Roger Kirk, whose niche is still empty. Anyone finding this body is eligible to receive a substantial fortune.

Babe yawned vaguely over this, but kept on reading because there was nothing else to do. Next was a thick sheet of business correspondence, bearing the letterhead of a firm of lawyers. The body of it ran:

In regard to your query regarding the will of Thaddeus Kirk, we are authorized to state that his grandfather was a man about five feet, five inches, whose left arm had been broken and who had a triangular silver plate set into his skull. There is no information as to the whereabouts of his death. He disappeared and was declared legally dead after the lapse of fourteen years.

The amount of the reward as stated in the will, plus accrued interest, now amounts to a fraction over $62,000. This will be paid to anyone who produces the remains, providing that said remains answer descriptions kept in our private files.

There was more, but Babe was bored. She went on to the little black notebook. There was nothing in it but penciled and highly abbreviated records of visits to libraries; quotations from books with titles like "History of Angelina and Tyler

Counties" and "Kirk Family History." Babe threw that aside, too. Where could Uncle Alton be?

She began to sing tunelessly, "Tumalumalum tum, ta ta ta," pretending to dance a minuet with flowering skirts like a girl she had seen in the movies. A rustle of the bushes at the entrance to The Place stopped her. She peeped upward, saw them being thrust aside. Quickly she ran to a tiny cul-de-sac in the rock wall, just big enough for her to hide in. She giggled at the thought of how surprised Uncle Alton would be when she jumped out at him.

She heard the newcomer, shuffling down the steep slope of the crevice and land heavily on the floor. There was something about the sound— What was it? It occurred to her that though it was a hard job for a big man like Uncle Alton to get through the little opening in the bushes, she could hear no heavy breathing. She heard no breathing at all!

Babe peeped out into the main cave and squealed in utmost horror. Standing there was, not Uncle Alton, but a massive caricature of a man: a huge thing like an irregular mud doll, clumsily made. It quivered and parts of it glistened and parts of it were dried and crumbly. Half of the lower left part of its face was gone, giving it a lopsided look. It had no perceptible mouth or nose, and its eyes were crooked, one higher than the other, both a dingy brown with no whites at all. It stood quite still looking at her, its only movement a steady unalive quivering.

It wondered about the queer little noise Babe had made.

Babe crept far back against a little pocket of stone, her brain running around and around in tiny circles of agony. She opened her mouth to cry out, and could not. Her eyes bulged and her face flamed with the strangling effort, and the two golden ropes of her braided hair twitched and twitched as she hunted hopelessly for a way out. If only she were out in the open—or in the wedge-shaped half-cave where the thing was—or home in bed!

The thing clumped toward her, expressionless, moving with a slow inevitability that was the sheer crux of horror. Babe lay wide-eyed and frozen, mounting pressure of terror stilling her lungs, making her heart shake the whole world. The monster came to the mouth of the little pocket, tried to walk to her and was stopped by the sides. It was such a narrow little fissure, and it was all Babe could do to get in. The thing from the woods stood straining against the rock at its shoulders, pressing harder and harder to get to Babe. She sat up slowly, so near to the thing that its odor was almost thick enough to see, and a wild hope burst through her voiceless fear. It couldn't get in! It couldn't get in because it was too big!

The substance of its feet spread slowly under the tremendous strain and at its shoulder appeared a slight crack. It widened as the monster unfeelingly crushed itself against the rock, and suddenly a large piece of the shoulder came away and the being twisted slushily three feet farther in. It lay quietly with its muddy eyes fixed on her, and then brought one thick arm up over its head and reached.

Babe scrambled in the inch farther she had believed impossible, and the filthy clubbed hand stroked down her back, leaving a trail of muck on the blue denim of the shirt she wore. The monster surged suddenly and, lying full length now, gained that last precious inch. A black hand seized one of her braids, and for Babe the lights went out.

When she came to, she was dangling by her hair from that same crusted paw. The thing held her high, so that her face and its featureless head were not more than a foot apart. It gazed at her with a mild curiosity in its eyes, and it swung her slowly back and forth. The agony of her pulled hair did what fear could not do—gave her a voice. She screamed. She opened her mouth and puffed up her powerful young lungs, and she sounded off. She held her throat in the position of the first scream, and her chest labored and pumped more air through the frozen throat. Shrill and monotonous and infinitely piercing, her screams.

The thing did not mind. It held her as she was, and watched. When it had learned all it could from this phenomenon, it dropped her jarringly, and looked around the half-cave, ignoring the stunned and huddled Babe. It reached over and picked up the leather briefcase and tore it twice across as if it were tissue. It saw the sandwich Babe had left, picked it up, crushed it, dropped it.

Babe opened her eyes, saw that she was free, and just as the thing turned back to her she dived between its legs and out in the shallow pool in front of the rock, paddled across and hit the other bank screaming. A vicious little light of fury burned in her; she picked up a grapefruit-sized stone and hurled it with all her frenzied might. It flew low and fast, and struck squashily on the monster's ankle. The thing was just taking a step toward the water; the stone caught it off balance, and its unpracticed equilibrium could not save it. It tottered for a long, silent moment at the edge and then splashed into the stream. Without a second look Babe ran shrieking away.

Cory Drew was following the little gobs of mold that somehow indicated the path of the murderer, and he was nearby when he first heard her scream. He broke into a run, dropping his shotgun and holding the .32-40 ready to fire. He ran with such deadly panic in his heart that he ran right past the huge cleft rock and was a hundred yards past it before she burst out through the pool and ran up the bank. He had to run hard and fast to catch her, because anything behind her was that faceless horror in the cave, and she was living for the one idea of getting away from there. He caught her in his arms and swung her to him, and she screamed on and on and on.

Babe didn't see Cory at all, even when he held her and quieted her.

The monster lay in the water. It neither liked nor disliked this new element. It rested on the bottom, its massive head a foot beneath the surface, and it curiously considered the facts that it had garnered. There was the little humming noise of Babe's voice that sent the monster questing into the cave. There was the black material of the briefcase that resisted so much more than green things when he tore it. There was the little two-legged one who sang and brought him near, and who screamed when he came. There was this new cold moving thing that he had fallen into. It was washing his body away. That had never happened before. That was interesting. The monster decided to stay and observe the new thing. It felt no urge to save itself; it could only be curious.

The brook came laughing down out of its spring, ran down from its source beckoning to the sunbeams and embracing freshets and helpful brooklets. It shouted and played with steaming little roots and nudged the minnows and pollywogs about in its tiny backwaters. It was a happy brook. When it came to the pool by the cloven rock it found the monster there, and plucked at it. It soaked the foul substances and smoothed and melted the molds, and the waters below the thing eddied darkly with its diluted matter. It was a thorough brook. It washed all it touched, persistently. Where it found filth, it removed filth; and if there were layer on layer of foulness, then layer by foul layer it was removed. It was a good brook. It did not mind the poison of the monster, but took it up and thinned it and spread it in little rings and around rocks downstream, and let it drift to the rootlets of water plants, that they might grow greener and lovelier. And the monster melted.

"I am smaller," the thing thought. "That is interesting. I could not move now. And now this part of me which thinks is going, too. It will stop in just a moment, and drift away with the rest of the body. It will stop thinking and I will stop being, and that, too, is a very interesting thing."

So the monster melted and dirtied the water, and the water was clean again, washing and washing the skeleton that the monster had left. It was not very big, and there was a badly healed knot on the left arm. The sunlight flickered on the triangular silver plate set into the pale skull, and the skeleton was very clean now. The brook laughed about it for an age.

They found the skeleton, six grim-lipped men who came to find a killer. No one had believed Babe, when she told her story days later. It had to be days later because Babe had screamed for seven hours without stopping, and had lain like a dead child for a day. No one believed her at all, because her story was all about the bad fella, and they knew that the bad fella was simply a thing that her father had made up to frighten her with. But it was through her that the skeleton was found, and so the men at the bank sent a check to the Drews for more money than they had ever dreamed about. It was old Roger Kirk, sure enough, that skeleton, though it was found five miles from where he had died and sank into the forest floor where the hot molds built around his skeleton and emerged—a monster.

So the Drews had a new barn and fine new livestock and they hired four men. But they didn't have Alton. And they didn't have Kimbo. And Babe screams at night and has grown very thin.

BEAUTY AND THE BEAST

Henry Kuttner

When we explore the other planets in our solar system, we may bring back seemingly innocuous things like the "jewel" from Venus in this story—really not a jewel at all, but an egg from which hatched a monstrous beast. And as the beast grew to adulthood, it had still more surprises for the people of Earth.

Henry Kuttner was one of the most popular writers of science fiction in the 1940's and 1950's, and is still so well remembered that an omnibus of his best stories was recently published. Beauty and the Beast *is one of his early tales, never before reprinted.*

Jared Kirth saw the meteor as he lay under the pines, staring up at the stars. He was on the verge of slumber, and the sleeping bag that wrapped his lean body was warm and comfortable.

Kirth was feeling well satisfied with himself, his stomach bulged with crisp, freshly caught trout, and there was still a week left of the fortnight's vacation he had allowed himself. So he lay quietly, watching the night sky, and the meteor shrieked its death agony in that last incandescent plunge through the atmosphere.

But before it went out of sight, the luminous body seemed to turn and arc in midair. That was queer enough. And even stranger was the shape of the thing, an elongated ovoid. Vaguely recalling that meteors sometimes contained precious ores, Kirth marked the spot where the flaming thunderbolt fell beyond a high ridge. And the next morning he shouldered his fishing tackle and hiked in that direction.

So he found the wrecked spaceship. It lay among the pines, a broken giant, its hull fused in many places by the heat of friction.

Kirth's pinched, rather mean mouth tightened as he looked down at the vessel. He was remembering that two months before a man named Jay Arden had left the Earth on the first interplanetary voyage.

Arden had been lost in space—so the papers had said. But now, apparently, his ship had returned, and Kirth's gaunt, gray-stubbled face was eager as he hastened down the slope.

He walked around the ship, slipping on sharp rocks and cursing once or twice before he found the port. But the metal surrounding it had fused and melted, so that entry was impossible at this point. The gray, pitted, rough metal of the craft defied the tentative ax-blows Kirth gave it. Curiosity mounted within him.

He examined the ship more closely. The sun, rising above the eastern ridge, showed a factor he had previously overlooked. There were windows, circular deadlights, so fused and burned that they were as opaque as the metallic hull. Yet they were unmistakably of glass or some similar substance.

It was not ordinary glass. It did not shatter under the ax. But a small chip flew, and Kirth battered away diligently until he had made a small hole. Vapor gushed out of this, foul, stale, and mephitic, and Kirth fell back and waited.

Then he returned to his labors. The glass was easier to shatter now, for some reason, and it was not long before Kirth had chopped away a hole large enough to permit the entry of his lean body. First, however, he took a small flashlight from his belt and held it at arm's length within the ship.

There was but one room, and this was a shambles. It was a mass of wreckage. Yet the air had cleared, and there seemed to be no danger. Cautiously Kirth squirmed through the deadlight.

So this was a spaceship! Kirth recognized the chamber from newspaper pictures he had seen months before.

In 1942 the ship had been new, shining, and perfect. Now, only a few months later, it was a ruin. The controls were hopelessly wrecked. Metal kits and canisters were scattered about the floor, broken straps on the walls showing whence they had fallen. And on the floor, too, lay the body of Jay Arden.

Kirth made a useless examination. The man was dead. His skin was blue and cyanosed, and his neck was obviously broken. Scattered about his corpse were a few cellulose-wrapped parcels that had spilled from a broken canister nearby. Through the transparent envelopes Kirth detected small black objects, smaller than peas, that resembled seeds.

Protruding from one of Arden's pockets was a notebook. As Kirth drew it forth, a wrapped parcel fell to the floor. Kirth hesitated, put the notebook aside, and opened the package.

Something fell from it into his palm. The man gasped in sheer wonder.

It was a jewel. Oval, large as an egg, the gem flamed gloriously in the light of the electric torch. It had no color, and yet seemed to partake of all the hues of the spectrum.

It seemed to draw into itself a thousand myriad hues—men would have died for such a jewel. Lovely it was, beyond imagination, and it was—unearthly.

Finally Kirth tore his gaze from the thing and opened the notebook. The light was too dim, so he carried it to the broken deadlight. Arden, seemingly, had not kept a diary, and his notes were broken and disconnected. But from the book, several photographs fluttered, and Kirth caught them as they fell.

The snapshots were blurred and discolored, but certain details showed with fair clarity. One showed a thick bar with rounded ends, white against blackness. This was a picture of the planet Venus, taken from outer space, though Kirth did not realize it. He examined the others.

Ruins. Cyclopean, strange, and alien in contour, half-destroyed shapes of stone were blurred against a dim background. One thing, however, was clear. The spaceship was visible in the picture—and Kirth gasped.

For the great ship was dwarfed by the gigantic ruins. Taller than the vast Temple of Karnak, monstrously large were the stones that had once been cities and buildings. Vague and murky as the pictures were, Kirth managed to form some conception of the gargantuan size of the structures shown in them. Too, he noticed that the geometry seemed oddly wrong. There were no stairs visible, only inclined planes. And a certain primeval crudeness, a lack of the delicacy noticeable even in the earlier Egyptian artifacts, was significant.

Most of the other photographs showed similar scenes. One, however, was different. It depicted a field of flowers, such flowers as Kirth had never before seen. Despite the lack of color, it was evident that the blossoms were lovely with a bizarre, unearthly beauty. Kirth turned to the notebook.

He learned something from it, though not much. He read: "Venus seems to be a dead planet. The atmosphere is breathable, but only plant life exists. The flowers, somewhat resembling orchids, are everywhere. The ground beneath them is covered with their seeds. I have collected a great many of these. . . .

"Since I found the jewel in one of the ruined structures, I have made another discovery. An intelligent race once lived

on Venus—the ruins themselves denote that fact. But any in-
scriptions they might have left have been long since eroded
by the foggy, wet atmosphere and the eternal rains. So I
thought, till this morning, when in a subterranean chamber I
discovered a bas-relief almost buried in mud.

"It took me hours to clear away the muck, and even then
there was not much to see. But the pictures are more
significant than any inscription in the ancient Venusian language could have been. I recognized, quite clearly, the jewel I
previously discovered. From what I have been able to make
out, there were many of these, artificially created. And they
were something more than mere gems.

"Unbelievable as it seems, they are—to use a familiar
parallel—eggs. There is life in them. Under the proper condi-
tions of heat and sunlight—so I interpret the bas-reliefs—they
will hatch. . . ."

There were a few other notes in the book, but these were
technical in nature and of no interest to Kirth, save for one
which mentioned the existence of a diary Arden had kept.
He again searched the ship, and this time found the diary.
But it was half incinerated by its proximity to the fused port,
and utterly illegible.

Pondering, Kirth examined the various containers. Some
were empty; others had dusty cinders in them and emitted a
burned, unpleasant odor when opened. The spoils of Arden's
voyage were, apparently, only the seeds and the jewel.

Now Jared Kirth, though shrewd, was not intelligent in
the true sense of the word. Born on a New England farm, he
had fought his way up by dint of hard, bitter persistence and
a continual insistence upon his own rights. As a result, he
owned a few farms and a small village store, and permitted
himself one brief vacation a year. On this furlough neither
his wife nor his daughter accompanied him. He was fifty, a
tall, spare, gray man, with cold eyes and a tight mouth that
was generally compressed as though in denial.

It is scarcely wonderful, therefore, that Kirth began to wonder how he might turn this discovery to serve his own ends. He knew that no reward had been offered for the finding of the spaceship, supposedly lost in the airless void. If there had been treasure of any sort in the vessel, he would have appropriated it, on the principle of "finder's keepers." There was nothing, save for the seeds and the gem, and Kirth had these in his pockets as he left the vessel.

The ship would not be found for some time, since this was wilderness country. Meanwhile, Kirth took with him Arden's notebook, to be destroyed at a more opportune moment. Though skeptical, he thought more than once of Arden's comparison of the jewel with an egg, and, for a man who owned several farms, the conclusion was inevitable. If this "egg" could be hatched, despite the unlikeliness of the idea, the result might be interesting. Even more—it might be profitable.

Kirth decided to cut short his vacation, and two days later he arrived at his home. He did not stay there, however, but went to one of his farms, taking with him his wife and daughter.

Heat and sunlight. A topless, electrically warmed incubator was the logical answer. At night, Kirth used a sunlamp on the jewel. Meanwhile, he waited.

Intrinsically the gem might have value. Kirth could, perhaps, have sold it for a large sum to some jeweler. But he thought better of this, and planted some of the Venusian seeds instead.

And, in the strange jewel, alien life stirred. Heat warmed it —heat that did not now exist on gloomy, rainswept Venus. From the sun poured energy, cosmic rays and other rays that for eons had been barred from the stone by the thick cloud barrier that shrouded Venus. Into the heart of the gem stole energy that set certain forces in motion. Life came, and dim realization.

There, on the straw of a filthy incubator, lay the visitant from another world. Unknown ages ago, it had been created, for a definite purpose. And now—life returned.

Kirth saw the hatching. At midday he stood beside the incubator, gnawing on a battered pipe, scratching the gray stubble on his jaw. His daughter was beside him, a lean, underfed girl of thirteen with sallow skin and hair.

"It ain't an egg, Pa," she said in a high, nasal voice. "You don't really expect that thing to hatch, do you?"

"Hush," Kirth grunted. "Don't keep pestering me. I—hey! Look at that thing! Something's—"

Something was indeed happening. On the straw the jewel lay, flaming bright. It seemed to suck sunlight into itself thirstily. The dim radiance that had come to surround it of late pulsed and waned—pulsed once more. The glow waxed—

Waxed brighter! An opaque cloud formed suddenly, hiding the gem. There came a high-pitched tinkling sound, almost above the threshold of hearing. It faded and was gone.

The gray mist fled. Where the jewel had been was nothing. Nothing, that is, save for a round, grayish ball that squirmed and shuddered weakly. . . .

"That ain't a chick," the girl said, her jaw hanging. "Pa—"
There was fright in her eyes.

"Hush!" Kirth said again. He bent down and gingerly prodded the thing. It seemed to writhe open, with an odd motion of uncoiling, and a tiny creature like a lizard lay there, its small mouth open as it sucked in air.

"I'll be damned," Kirth said slowly. "A dirty little lizard!" He felt vaguely sick. The jewel he might have sold at a good price, but this creature—what could be done with it? Who could want it?

Yet it was strange enough. It was shaped like a miniature

kangaroo, almost, and like no lizard Kirth had ever seen before. Perhaps he might sell it after all.

"Go git a box," he said to his daughter, and, when she had obeyed, he picked up the reptile gingerly and deposited it in the impromptu prison.

As he carried it into the house, he glanced at the plot of ground where he had planted some of the seeds. A few yellowish, small spears were sprouting up. Kirth nodded approvingly and scratched his jaw.

Mrs. Kirth, a plump, slatternly woman, approached. Her face was prematurely old, sagging in fat wrinkles. Her brown eyes had a defeated look, though there was still something of beauty in them.

"What you got there, Jay?" she asked.

"Tell you later," he said. "Git me some milk, Nora. And an eyedropper or something."

This was done. Kirth fed the reptile, which seemed to like the milk and sucked it down greedily. Its small, glittering eyes stared up unwinkingly.

"Pa," the girl said. "It's bigger. Lots bigger."

"Couldn't be," Kirth said. "Things don't grow that fast. Git out, now, and leave me be."

And in its prison the tiny creature that was to become the Beast drank thirstily of the milk, while in the dim, alien brain, clouded by the mists of centuries, thoughts began to stir. The first faint chords of memory vibrated . . . memory of a previous life, half forgotten. . . .

Kirth's daughter had been right. The reptile grew, abnormally and alarmingly. At the end of the second day, it was six inches long from blunt muzzle to tapering tail. When the week was over, it was more than twice as large. Kirth built a pen for it and was secretly elated.

"I can sell it, all right," he exulted. "Some circus'd pay me plenty. But it might git even bigger. I'll wait a bit."

Meanwhile he tended his Venusian plants. They were sprouting most satisfactorily now, and the beginnings of buds were evident. They were as tall as hollyhocks, but leafless. The thick, rigid stem, pale yellow in hue, was studded with swellings that presently burst into bloom.

At the end of the second week Kirth's garden was a riot of color, and he paid a photographer to take snapshots in color. These he sent to several horticultural gardens, which were immediately interested. A reporter got on the trail and interviewed Kirth.

Kirth was wary and spoke of plant grafting and experiments he had made. A new species of flower it was, and he had grown them. Yes, he had some seeds, and would sell them. . . .

The wrecked spaceship had not yet been discovered. And in its sty the Beast ate enormously of vegetables, and of swill which Kirth refused the reluctant hogs, and drank anything it could get. A scientist would have known, by the shape of the Beast's teeth, that it was carnivorous or at least omnivorous, but Kirth did not know, and the reptile did not appear to object to its menu. It grew, remarkably, and its basal metabolism was so high that its scaly body emitted perceptible heat.

It was as large now as a stallion. But it seemed so gentle that Kirth took no warning, though he kept a revolver in his pocket whenever he approached his bizarre charge.

The dim memories within the Beast's brain stirred into life from time to time. But one factor predominated, drowning them and lulling them to slumber. The Beast knew, somehow, that it was necessary for him to grow. Before anything else, he must attain his full growth and maturity. After that—

The Beast was intelligent, not with the aptitude of a child, but with the mind of a half-drugged adult. And he was not born of Earth. The alien chemistry of his body sent unknown secretions coursing through his veins, and, as he ate and grew, that strange mind worked. . . .

The Beast learned, though as yet he could not take advantage of his knowledge. The Kirths' conversation was clearly audible to him through the open windows of the farmhouse, and their televisor was very often turned on. From observing the humans, he grew to recognize their moods, and in turn came to associate certain word-sounds with those moods.

He learned that certain grimaces accompanied a special set of emotions. He grew to understand laughter and tears.

One thing he did not understand—a look that came into the eyes of Mrs. Kirth and her daughter, and sometimes into Kirth's eyes, as they watched him. It was repugnance and horror, but the Beast did not know that.

Two months passed slowly. Kirth received many checks in his mail. The new flowers had proved tremendously popular, and florists demanded them avidly. Lovelier than orchids they were, and they did not fade for a long time after being cut.

Kirth was not shrewd enough to keep control of the plants in his own hands, and the distribution of them got beyond him. Since the flowers would flourish in any climate, they were grown from California to New York. Fields of them formed a carpet of beauty over America. The fad spread over the world, and in Buenos Aires, London, and Berlin no socialite attended a *dansant* without a corsage of the Rainbows, as the blooms came to be called.

Kirth might have been satisfied with his growing bank account, but he had already got in touch with the owners of several circuses and told them he had a freak to sell. Kirth was becoming apprehensive. The Beast was uncomfortably huge, and people were noticing that scaled, swaying back as it moved about. Kirth, with some trepidation, led the monster into the barn, though it followed willingly enough. But the quarters were cramped. One blow from the mighty tail would have wrecked the structure, and that was scarcely a pleasant thought.

Kirth would have been even more disturbed had he realized what was going on in the monster's brain. The fogs were dissipating as the Beast approached swift maturity. Intelligence and memory were returning. And already the creature could understand many English words.

That was natural enough. A child does the same, over a period of years, by a process of association, experiment, and mental retention of word-sounds. The Beast was not a child. He was a highly intelligent being, and for months he had been in close contact with human beings. At times, he found it hard to concentrate, and would devote himself to feeding and sleeping, in a dull, pleasantly languorous stupor. Then the driving, inexorable force within him would awaken him to life once more.

It was hard to remember. The metamorphosis he had undergone had altered the psychic patterns of his mind to some degree. But one day he saw, through a crack in the barn, the Venusian flowers, and by a natural process of association thought of long-forgotten things. Then a dull, gray, rainy day occurred. . . .

Rain. Chill, bleak water that splashed on his scaled hide. Thick fogs, through which structures reared. And among those stone buildings moved beings like himself. The Beast remembered. . . .

The hideous, armored head swayed in the dimness of the barn. The saucer eyes stared into vacancy. Tremendous and frightful, the Beast crouched, while its thoughts went far and far into the dusty ages of the past.

Others. There had been others like itself, the ruling race of the second planet. Something had happened. Death . . . doom. Many had died. All over the rain-swept, twilit world the mighty reptiles had perished. Nothing could save them from the plague that had come from outer space.

The vast hulk shuddered uneasily in the gloom.

No escape. Yes, there had been one. Despite the beast form of the creatures, they had been intelligent. And they had possessed science of a kind. It was not Earthly science—but it had found an escape.

Not in their own form. Nothing could protect the huge reptilian bodies from the plague. But in another form . . . a form in which the basic energy patterns of their bodies would remain unaltered, though compressed by the creation of atomic stasis . . .

Matter is not solid. Bodies are formed of incredibly tiny solar systems, electrons that swing in wide orbits about their protons. Under the influence of cold this submicroscopic motion is slowed down, and at the point of absolute zero it ceases. But absolute zero means the cessation of all energy, and is impossible.

Impossible? Not on Venus, ages ago. As an experiment the life energy had been drained from one of the reptiles. As the electrons drew in toward their protons, there had been a shrinkage . . . and a change. A jewel of frozen life, an entity held in absolute stasis, lay before the Venusian scientists, waiting for the heat and solar rays that would waken it to life once more.

Space travel, to those bulky and gigantic forms, was impossible. But if, in different guise, they could flee to another, safer world. . . .

That had been the plan. All the energies of the Venusian survivors were turned toward constructing a spaceship. In this vessel the life-gems were to be stored and, as soon as possible, automatic robot controls would guide the craft across space, to Earth. Once a safe landing had been effected, other robot apparatus would expose the jewels to sunlight and heat, and the

Venusians would live again after their cataleptic voyage across the void. But the plan had not been completed. The plague was too deadly. The spaceship's unfinished ruins still lay hidden deep in a Venusian swamp, and it had been an Earthman, after all, who had brought one of the strange jewels to his own world.

All over Venus the gems were hidden. The Beast had seen the night sky and learned that he was on the third planet. That meant he had been brought here from his own world, and revivified by the energizing rays. He felt gratitude to the Earthmen who had rescued him from the eternal life-in-death.

Perhaps he was not the only one. Perhaps others of his race existed here, on Earth. Well, he would communicate with these humans, now that the fogs were clearing from his brain. Strange creatures they were, bipeds, and hideous to the Beast's alien eyes. But he was grateful to them, nevertheless.

How could he communicate? The Earthmen were intelligent, that was evident enough. His own language would be incomprehensible to them, and though he could understand English after a fashion, his throat and tongue could not form recognizable words. Well, mathematics was a universal language, and that could be the beginning. There was something he must tell Earthmen—something vitally important. But they were the ruling race on this planet, and it would not be too difficult to establish communication with them.

The Beast moved clumsily. His body lurched against the wall of the barn and, with a crackling crash, timbers gave way. The big structures sagged down, and as the Beast drew back in dismay, he completed the job of ruin. He stood amid the wreck of something that no longer resembled a barn. Impatiently, he shook it off. Things on this world were delicate indeed. The heavy stone structures of Venus were built to withstand normal shocks.

The noise had been heard. Kirth came running out of the farmhouse, carrying a shotgun and holding an electric torch. His wife was beside him. They started toward the barn, and then paused, apprehensive.

"It—it tore it down," Mrs. Kirth said stupidly. "Do you think it'll— Jay! Wait!"

But Kirth went forward, holding the gun ready. In the moonlight the gross bulk of the monster loomed hideously above him.

And the Beast thought: It is time. Time to establish communication. . . .

A huge foreleg lifted and began to trace a design in the dirt of the farmyard. A circle formed, and another. In time, a map of the solar system was clear.

"Look at the way it's pawing," Mrs. Kirth said. "Like a bull getting ready to charge. Jay—watch out!"

"I'm watching," Kirth said grimly. And he lifted the gun.

The Beast drew back, without fear, but waiting for the man to see the design. Yet Kirth's eyes saw only a meaningless maze of concentric circles. He walked slowly forward, his boots obliterating the design.

"He did not notice it," the Beast thought. "I must try again. Surely it will be easy to make him understand. In such a highly organized civilization, only a scientist would have been entrusted with my care."

Remembering the gesture of greeting among Earthmen, the Beast lifted a foreleg and slowly extended it. Shaking hands was fantastically impossible, but Kirth would recognize the significance of the motion.

Instead, Kirth fired. The bullet ripped along the Beast's skull, a painful though not dangerous wound. The Beast instantly withdrew its paw.

The man did not understand. Perhaps it thought harm had been offered, had read menace in the friendly gesture. The Beast lowered its head in a motion of submission.

At sight of that frightful mask swooping down, Mrs. Kirth broke through her paralysis of terror. She shrieked in an agony of fear and turned to flee. Kirth, yelling hysterical oaths, pumped bullet after bullet at the reptile.

The Beast turned clumsily. It was not hurt, but there was danger here. Attempting to escape without damaging the frail structures all around, it managed to step on a pigsty, ruin a silo, and crush in one wall of the farmhouse.

But this could not be helped. The Beast retreated and was lost in the night.

The inhuman brain was puzzled. What had gone wrong now? Earthmen were intelligent, yet they had not understood. Perhaps the fault lay with itself. Full maturity had not been reached; the thought-patterns were still not set in their former matrices. The fogs that shrouded the reptile's mind were not yet completely dissipated. . . .

Growth! Maturity! That was necessary. Once maturity had been achieved, the Beast could meet Earthmen on equal terms and make them understand. But food was necessary. . . .

The Beast lumbered on through the moonlit gloom. It went like a behemoth through fences and plowed fields, leaving a swathe of destruction in its wake. At first it tried to keep to roads, but the concrete and asphalt were shattered beneath the vast weight. So it gave up that plan, and headed for the distant mountains.

A shouting grew behind it. Red light flared. Searchlights began to sweep the sky. But this tumult died as the Beast drove farther and farther into the mountains. For a time, it must avoid men. It must concentrate on—food!

The Beast liked the taste of flesh, but it also understood the rights of property. Animals were owned by men. Therefore they must not be molested. But plants—cellulose—almost anything was fuel for growth. Even the limbs of trees were digestible.

So the colossus roamed the wilderness. Deer and cougars it caught and ate, but mostly vegetation. Once, it saw an airplane droning overhead, and after that more planes came, dropping bombs. But after sundown, the Beast managed to escape.

It grew unimaginably. Some effect of the sun's actinic rays, not filtered as on cloud-veiled Venus, made the Beast grow far beyond the size it had been on Venus eons ago. It grew larger than the vastest dinosaur that ever stalked through the swamps of Earth's dawn, a titanic, nightmare juggernaut out of the Apocalypse. It looked like a walking mountain. And, inevitably, it became clumsier.

The pull of gravity was a serious handicap. Walking was painful work. Climbing slopes, dragging its huge body, was agony. No more could the Beast catch deer. They fleetly evaded the ponderous movements.

Inevitably, such a creature could not escape detection. More planes came, with bombs. The Beast was wounded again, and realized the necessity of communicating with Earthmen without delay. Maturity had been reached. . . .

There was something of vital importance that Earthmen must know. Life had been given to the Beast by Earthmen, and that was a debt to be repaid.

The Beast came out of the mountains. It came by night, and traveled swiftly, searching for a city. There, it knew, was the best chance of finding understanding. The giant's stride shook the earth as it thundered through the dark.

On and on it went. So swift was its progress that the bombers did not find it till dawn. Then the bombs fell, and more than one found its mark.

But the wounds were superficial. The Beast was a mighty, armored Juggernaut, and such a thing may not be easily slain. It felt a pain, however, and moved faster. The men in the sky, riding their air-chariots, did not understand—but somewhere would be men of science. Somewhere. . . .

And so the Beast came to Washington.

Strangely, it recognized the Capitol. Yet it was, perhaps, natural, for the Beast had learned English, and had listened to Kirth's televisor for months. Descriptions of Washington had been broadcast, and the Beast knew that this was the center of government in America. Here, if anywhere on Earth, there would be men who understood. Here were the rulers, the wise men. And despite its wounds, the Beast felt a thrill of exultation as it sped on.

The planes dived thunderously. The aerial torpedoes screamed down. Crashing they came, ripping flesh from that titanic armored body.

"It's stopped!" said a pilot, a thousand feet above the Beast. "I think we've killed it! Thank God it didn't get into the city—"

The Beast stirred into slow movement. The fires of pain bathed it. The reptilian nerves sent their unmistakable messages to the brain, and the Beast knew it had been wounded unto death. Strangely it felt no hate for the men who had slain it.

No—they could not be blamed. They had not known. And, after all, humans had taken the Beast from Venus, restored it to life, tended and fed it for months. . . .

And there was still a debt. There was a message that Earthmen must know. Before the Beast died, it must convey that message, somehow.

The saucer eyes saw the white dome of the Capitol in the distance. There could be found science, and understanding. But it was so far away!

The Beast rose. It charged forward. There was no time to consider the fragility of the man-made structures all around. The message was more important.

The bellow of thunder marked the Beast's progress. Clouds

of ruin rose up from toppling buildings. Marble and granite were not the iron-hard stone of Venus, and a trail of destruction led toward the Capitol. The planes followed in uncertainty. They dared not loose bombs above Washington.

Near the Capitol was a tall derricklike tower. It had been built for the accommodation of newscasters and photographers, but now it served a different purpose. A machine had been set up there hastily, and men frantically worked connecting power cables. A lens-shaped projector, gleaming in the sunlight, was swinging slowly to focus on the oncoming monster. It resembled a great eye, high above Washington.

It was a heat ray.

It was one of the first in existence, and if it could not stop the reptile, nothing could.

Still the Beast came on. Its vitality was going fast, but there would still be time. Time to convey its message to the men in the Capitol, the men who would understand.

From doomed Washington arose a cry, from ten thousand panic-strained throats. In the streets men and women fought and struggled and fled from the oncoming monster that towered against the sky, colossal and horrible.

On the tower soldiers worked at the projector, connecting, tightening, barking sharp orders.

The Beast halted. It paused before the Capitol. From the structure, men were fleeing. . . .

The fogs were creeping up to shroud the reptile brain. The Beast fought against increasing lassitude. The message—the message!

A mighty forepaw reached out. The Beast had forgotten Earth's gravity, and the clumsiness of its own gross bulk.

The massive paw crashed through the Capitol's dome!

Simultaneously the heat ray flashed out blindly. It swept up and bathed the Beast in flaming brilliance.

For a heartbeat the tableau held, the colossus towering above the nation's Capitol. Then the Beast fell. . . .

In death, it was terrible beyond imagination. The heat ray crumpled it amid twisted iron girders. The Capitol itself was shattered into utter ruin. For blocks buildings collapsed, and clouds of dust billowed up in a thick, shrouding veil.

The clouds were blinding, like the mists that darkened the sight and the mind of the Beast. For the reptile was not yet dead. Unable to move, the life ebbing swiftly from it, the Beast yet strove to stretch out one monstrous paw. . . .

Darkly it thought: I must give them the message. I must tell them of the plague that destroyed all life on Venus. I must tell them of the virus, borne on the winds, against which there is no protection. Out of space, it came to Venus, spores that grew to flowers. And now, the flowers grow on Earth. In a month, the petals will fall, and from the blossoms the virus will develop. And then, all life on Earth will be destroyed, as it was on Venus, and nothing will exist on all the planet but bright flowers and the ruins of cities. I must warn them to destroy the blossoms now, before they pollinate. . . .

The mists were very thick now. The Beast shuddered convulsively, and lay still. It was dead.

On a rooftop, a man and a woman watched from the distance. The man said: "God, what a horrible thing! Look at it lying there, like the devil himself." He shuddered and glanced away.

The white-faced woman nodded. "It's hard to believe the world can hold so much horror, and yet can give us anything as beautiful as this. . . ." Her slim fingers stroked the velvety petals of the blossom that was pinned to her dress. Radiant, lovely, the flower from Venus glowed in the sunlight.

Already, pollen was forming within its cup.

SOME ARE BORN CATS

Terry and Carol Carr

*If creatures from another star wanted to visit Earth in se-
cret, perhaps they could do it by changing their shapes so that
they'd look like the everyday life-forms we're used to seeing
. . . such as cats. But even if the aliens could make themselves look like cats, how would they know how to act? And a
cat that doesn't act like a cat is very conspicuous. . . .*

*Carol and I have been married for a long time, and we've
each written science fiction stories, but* Some Are Born Cats
*was the first one we wrote together. Perhaps that's the reason
this story is one of our favorites.*

"Maybe he's an alien shape-changing spy from Arcturus,"
Freddie said.

"What does that mean?" asked the girl.

Freddie shrugged. "Maybe he's not a cat at all. He could
be some kind of alien creature that came to Earth to spy on
us. He could be hiding in the shape of a cat while he studies
us and sends back reports to Arcturus or someplace."

She looked at the cat, whose black body lay draped across
the top of the television set, white muzzle on white paws,
wide green eyes open and staring at them. The boy and the
girl lay on her bed, surrounded by schoolbooks.

"You're probably right," she said. "He gives me the
creeps."

The girl's name was Alyson, and it was her room. She and Freddie spent a lot of their time together, though it wasn't a real Thing between them. Nothing official, nor even unofficial. They'd started the evening doing homework together, but now they were watching "Creature Features," with the sound turned down.

"He always does that," Alyson said. "He gets up on the television set whenever there's a scary movie on, and he drapes his tail down the side like that and just *stares* at me. I'm watching a vampire movie, and I happen to glance up and there he is, looking at me. He never blinks, even. It really freaks me out sometimes."

The cat sat up suddenly, blinking. It yawned and began an elaborate washing of its face. White paws, white chest, white face, and the rest of him was raven black. With only the television screen illuminating the room, he seemed to float in the darkness. On the screen now was a commercial for campers; a man who looked Oriental was telling them that campers were the best way to see America.

"What kind of a name is Gilgamesh?" Freddie asked. "That's his name, isn't it?"

"It's ancient Babylonian or something like that," Alyson told him. "He was kind of a god; there's a whole long story about him. I just liked the name, and he looked so scraggly and helpless when he adopted us, I thought maybe he could use a fancy name. But most of the time I just call him Gil anyway."

"Is George short for anything?" the boy asked. George was her other cat, a placid Siamese. George was in some other part of the house.

"No, he's just George. He looks so elegant, I didn't think he needed a very special name."

"Gilgamesh, you ought to pay more attention to George," the boy said. "He's a *real* cat; he acts like a cat would really

act. You don't see *him* sitting on top of horror shows and act-
ing weird."

"George gets up on the television set too, but he just goes
to sleep," Alyson said.

The cat, Gilgamesh, blinked at them and slowly lay down
again, spreading himself carefully across the top of the TV
set. He didn't look at them.

"Do you mean Gil could be just hypnotizing us to think
he's a cat?" Alyson asked. "Or do you suppose he took over
the body of a real cat when he arrived here on Earth?"

"Either way," Freddie said. "It's how he acts that's the tip-
off. He doesn't act like a cat would. Hey, Gil, you really
ought to study George—he knows what it's all about."

Gilgamesh lay still, eyes closed. They watched the movie,
and after it, the late news. An announcer jokingly reported
that strange lights had been seen in the skies over Watsonville, and he asked the TV weatherman if he could explain
them. The weatherman said, "We may have a new wave of
flying saucers moving in from the Pacific." Everybody in the
studio laughed.

Gilgamesh jumped off the television set and left the room.

Freddie's Saturday morning began at eight o'clock with the
"World News Roundup of the Week." He opened one eye
cautiously and saw an on-the-spot reporter interviewing the
families of three sky divers whose parachutes had failed to
open.

Freddie was about to go downstairs for breakfast when the
one woman reporter in the group smilingly announced that
Friday night, at 11:45 P.M., forty-two people had called the
studio to report a flying-saucer sighting. One man, the owner
of a fish store, referred to "a school of saucers." The news
team laughed, but Freddie's heartbeat quickened.

It took him twenty minutes to get through to Alyson, and

when she picked up the phone, he was caught unprepared, with a mouthful of English muffin.

"Hello? Hello?"

"Mmgfghmf."

"Hello? Who *is* this?"

"Chrglfmhph."

"Oh, my goodness! Mom! I think it's one of those obscene calls!" She sounded deliriously happy. But she hung up.

Freddie swallowed and dialed again.

"Boy, am I glad it's you," Alyson said. "Listen, you've got to come right over—it's been one incredible thing after another ever since you left last night. First, the saucers—did you hear about them?—and then Gil freaking out, then a real creepy obscene telephone call."

"Hold it, hold it," Freddie said. "I'll meet you back of the house in five minutes."

When he got there, Alyson was lying stomach down on the lawn, chewing a blade of grass. She looked only slightly more calm than she sounded.

"Freddie," she said almost tragically. "How much do you know?"

"About as much as the next guy."

"No, seriously—I mean about the saucers last night. Did you see them?"

"I was asleep. Did you?"

"*See* them! I practically *touched* them." She looked deep into his eyes. "But Freddie, that's not the important part."

"What is? What?"

"Gilgamesh. I seriously believe he's having a nervous breakdown. I hate to think of what else it could be." She got up. "Wait right here. I want you to see this."

Freddie waited, a collage of living-color images dancing in his head: enemy sky divers, a massacred school of flying saucers, shape-changing spies from Arcturus. . . .

Alyson came back holding a limp Gilgamesh over her arm.

"He was in the litter pan," she said significantly. "He was covering it up."

"Covering what up?"

"His doo-doo, silly."

Freddie winced. There were moments when he wished Alyson were a bit more liberated.

Gilgamesh settled down on Alyson's lap and purred frantically.

"He has *never*, not once before, covered it up," she insisted. "He always gets out of the box when he's finished and scratches on the floor near it. George comes along eventually and does it for him."

Gilgamesh licked one paw and applied it to his right ear. It was a highly adorable action, one that never failed to please. He did it twice more—lick, tilt head, rub; lick, tilt head, rub —then stopped and looked at Freddie out of the corner of his eye.

"You see what I mean?" Alyson said. "Do you know what that look means?"

"He's asking for approval," said Freddie. "No doubt about it. He wants to know if he did it right."

"Exactly!"

Gilgamesh tucked his head between his white paws and closed his eyes.

"He feels that he's a failure," Alyson interpreted.

"Right."

Gilgamesh turned over on his back, let his legs flop, and began to purr. His body trembled like a lawn mower standing still.

Freddie nodded. "Overdone. Everything he does is self-conscious."

"And you know when he's not self-conscious? When he's staring. But he doesn't look like a cat then, either."

"What did he do last night, when the saucers were here?"

Alyson sat up straight; Gilgamesh looked at her suspiciously.

"He positively freaked," she said. "He took one look and his tail bushed out and he arched his back. . . ."

"That's not so freaky. Any kind of cat would do that."

"I know . . . it's what comes next." She paused dramatically. "In the middle of this bushy-tailed fit, he stopped dead in his tracks, shook his head, and trotted into the house to find George. Gil woke him up and chased him onto the porch. Then you know what he did? He put a paw on George's shoulder, like they were old buddies. And you know how George is—he just went along with it; he'll groove on anything. But it was so weird. George wanted to leave, but Gil kept him there by washing him. George can't resist a wash—he's too busy grooving to do it himself—so he stayed till the saucers took off."

Freddie picked up Alyson's half-chewed blade of grass and put it in his mouth. "You think that Gil, for reasons of his own, manipulated George into watching saucers with him?"

Gilgamesh stopped being a lawn mower long enough to bat listlessly at a bumblebee. Then he looked at Alyson slyly and resumed his purring.

"That's exactly what I think. What do you think?"

Freddie thought about it for a while, gazing idly at Gilgamesh. The cat avoided his eyes.

"Why would he want George to watch flying saucers with him?" Freddie asked.

Alyson shrugged elaborately, tossing her hair and looking at the clear blue of the sky. "*I* don't know. Flying saucers are spaceships, aren't they? Maybe Gilgamesh came here in one of them."

"But why would he want *George* to look at one?"

"I'll tell you what," said Alyson. "Why don't you ask Gilgamesh about that?"

Freddie glanced again at the cat; Gilgamesh was lying preternaturally still, as though asleep, yet too rigid to be truly asleep. Playing 'possum, Freddie thought. Listening.

"Hey, Gil," he said softly. "Why did you want George to see the flying saucers?"

Gilgamesh made no acknowledgment that he had heard. But Freddie noticed that his tail twitched.

"Come on, Gil, you can tell *me*," he coaxed. "I'm from Procyon, myself."

Gilgamesh sat bolt upright, eyes wide and shocked. Then he seemed to recollect himself, and he swatted at a nonexistent bee, chased his tail in a circle, and ran off around the corner of the house.

"You nearly got him that time," Alyson said. "That line about being from Procyon blew his mind."

"Next time we tie him to a chair and hang a naked light bulb over his head," Freddie said.

After school Monday, Freddie stopped off at the public library and did a little research. They kept files of the daily newspapers there, and Freddie spent several hours checking through the papers for the last several months for mentions of flying saucers or anything else unusual.

That evening, in Alyson's room, Freddie said, "Let's skip the French vocabulary for a while. When did you get Gilgamesh?"

Alyson had George on her lap; the placid Siamese lay like a dead weight except for his low-grade purr. Alyson said, "Three weeks ago. Gil just wandered into the kitchen, and we thought he was a stray—I mean, he couldn't have belonged to anybody, because he was so dirty and thin, and anyway, he didn't have a collar."

"Three weeks ago," Freddie said. "What day, exactly?"

She frowned, thinking back. "Mmm . . . it was a Tuesday. Three weeks ago tomorrow, then."

"That figures," Freddie said. "Alyson, do you know what

happened the day before Gilgamesh just walked into your life?"

She stared wonderingly at him for a moment, then something lit in her eyes. "That was the night the sky was so loud!"

"Yes," said Freddie.

Alyson sat up on the bed, shedding both George and the books from her lap in her excitement. "And then that Tuesday we asked Mr. Newcomb in science class what had caused it, and he just said a lot of weird stuff that didn't mean anything, remember? Like he really didn't know, but he was a teacher, and he thought he had to be able to explain everything."

"Right," said Freddie. "An unexplainable scientific phenomenon in the skies, and the next day Gilgamesh just happened to show up on your doorstep. I'll bet there were flying saucers that night, too, only nobody saw them."

George sleepily climbed back onto the bed and settled down in Alyson's lap again. She idly scratched his ear, and he licked her hand, then closed his eyes and went to sleep again.

"You think it was flying saucers that made all those weird noises in the sky?" Alyson asked.

"Sure," he said. "Probably. Especially if that was the night before Gilgamesh got here. I wonder what his mission is?"

"What?" said Alyson.

"I wonder why he's here, on Earth. Do you think they're really planning to invade us?"

"Who?" she asked. "You mean people from flying saucers? Oh, Freddie, cool it. I mean a joke's a joke, and Gilgamesh *is* pretty creepy, but he's only a little black-and-white cat. He's not some invader from Mars!"

"Arcturus," Freddie said. "Or maybe it's really Procyon; maybe that's why he was so startled when I said that yesterday."

"Freddie! He's a *cat!*"

"You think so?" Freddie asked. "Let me show you something about your innocent little stray cat."

He got off the bed and silently went to the door of the bedroom. Grasping the knob gently, he suddenly threw the door open wide.

Standing right outside the door was Gilgamesh. The black-and-white cat leaped backward, then quickly recovered himself and walked calmly into the room, as though he had just been on his way in when the door opened. But Freddie saw that his tail was fully bushed out.

"You still think he's a cat?" Freddie asked.

"Freddie, he's just a little weird, that's all—"

"*Weird?* This cat's so weird he's probably got seven hearts and an extra brain in his back! Alyson, this is no ordinary cat!"

Gilgamesh jumped up on the bed, studied how George was lying, and arranged himself in a comparable position next to Alyson. She petted him for a moment, and he began to purr his odd high-pitched purr.

"You think he's just a cat?" Freddie asked. "He sounds like a cricket."

"Freddie, are you serious?" Alyson said. Freddie nodded. He'd done his research at the library, and he was sure something strange was going on.

"Well, then," said Alyson. "I know what we can do. We'll take him to my brother and see if he's really a cat or not."

"Your brother? But he's a chiropractor."

Alyson smiled. "But he has an X-ray machine. We'll *see* if Gilgamesh really has those extra hearts and all."

On her lap, George continued to purr. Next to her, Gilgamesh seemed to have developed a tic in the side of his face, but he continued to lie still.

Alyson's brother, the chiropractor, had his office in the Watsonville Shopping Center, next door to the Watsonville

Bowling Alley. His receptionist told them to wait in the anteroom, the doctor would be with them in a moment.

Alyson and Freddie sat down on a black sofa, with the carrying case between them. From inside the case came pitiful mews and occasional thrashings about. From inside the office came sounds of pitiful cries and the high notes of Beethoven's Fifth. Somebody made a strike next door; the carrying case flew a foot into the air. Freddie transferred it to his lap and held it steady.

A young man with longish brown hair and a white jacket opened the door.

"Hey sister, hi Freddie. What's happening?"

Alyson pointed to the carrying case. "This is the patient I told you about, Bob."

"Okay. Let's go in and take a look."

He opened the case. Gilgamesh had curled himself into a tight ball of fur, his face pressed against the corner. When the doctor lifted him out, Freddie saw that the cat's eyes were clenched shut.

"I've never seen him so terrified," Alyson said. "Weird, freaky, yes, but never this scared."

"I still don't understand why you didn't take him to a vet if you think he's sick," her brother said.

Alyson grinned ingratiatingly. "You're cheaper."

"Hmpf."

All this time the doctor had been holding the rigid Gilgamesh in the air. As soon as he put him down on the examining table, the cat opened his eyes to twice their normal size, shot a bushy tail straight up, and dashed under the table. He cowered there, face between paws. Alyson's brother crawled under the table, but the cat scrambled to the opposite side of the room and hid behind a rubber plant. Two green eyes peeked through the leaves.

"I think stronger measures are indicated," the doctor said.

He opened a drawer and removed a hypodermic needle and a small glass bottle.

Freddie and Alyson approached the rubber plant from each end, then grabbed.

Freddie lifted the cat onto the examining table. Gilgamesh froze, every muscle rigid—but his eyes darted dramatically around the room, looking for escape.

The doctor gave him the shot, and within seconds he was a boneless pussycat who submitted docilely to the indignities of being X-rayed in eight different positions.

Ten minutes later Alyson's brother announced the results— no abnormalities; Gilgamesh was a perfectly healthy cat.

"Does he have any extra hearts?" Alyson said. "Anything funny about his back?"

"He's completely normal," said her brother. "Doesn't even have any extra toes." He saw the worried expression on her face. "Wasn't that what you wanted to find out?"

"Sure," said Alyson. "Thanks a lot. I'm really relieved."

"Me, too," said Freddie. "Very."

Neither of them looked it.

"Lousy job," said Gilgamesh.

They turned to look at him, mouths open. The cat's mouth was closed. He was vibrating like a lawn mower again, purring softly.

Freddie looked at the doctor. "Did someone just say something?"

"Somebody just said, 'Lousy job,'" said the doctor. "I thought it was your cat. I must be losing my mind. Alyson?" She looked to be in shock. "Did you hear anything?"

"No. I didn't hear him say 'Lousy job' or anything like that." Still in a daze, she went over to the cat and stroked him on the head. Then she bent down and whispered something in his ear.

"Just haven't got the knack," said Gilgamesh. "Crash

course." He smiled, closed his eyes, and fell asleep. But there was no doubt that it was he who had spoken.

Freddie, who had just got over the first wave of disbelief, said, "What was in that injection, anyway?"

"Sodium pentothal. Very small dose. I think I'd better sit down." The doctor staggered to the nearest chair, almost missing it.

"Hey, Alyson?" the doctor said.

"Huh?"

"Maybe you'd better tell me why you really brought your cat in here."

"Well," said Alyson.

"Come on, little sister, give," he said.

Alyson looked at the floor and mumbled, "Freddie thinks he's a spy from outer space."

"From Arcturus," said Freddie.

"Procyon," said Gilgamesh. He yawned and rolled onto his side.

"Wait a minute," said the doctor. "Wait a minute, I want to get something straight." But he just stared at the cat, at Freddie, at Alyson.

Freddie took advantage of the silence. "Gilgamesh, you were just talking, weren't you?"

"Lemme sleep," Gilgamesh mumbled.

"What's your game, Gil?" Freddie asked him. "Are you spying on us? You're really some shapeless amoeba-like being that can rearrange its protoplasm at will, aren't you? Are your people planning to invade Earth? When will the first strike hit? Come on, *talk!*"

"Lemme sleep," Gilgamesh said.

Freddie picked up the cat and held him directly under the fluorescent light of the examining table. Gilgamesh winced and squirmed, feebly.

"Talk!" Freddie commanded. "Tell us the invasion plans."

"No invasion," Gilgamesh whined. "Lemme down. No fair drugging me."

"Are you from Procyon?" Freddie asked him.

"Are you from Killarney?" the cat sang, rather drunkenly. "Studied old radio broadcasts, sorry. Sure, from Procyon. Tried to act like a cat but couldn't get the hang of it. Never can remember what to do with my tail."

"What are you doing on Earth?" Freddie demanded.

"Chasing a runaway," the cat mumbled. "Antisocial renegade, classified for work camps. Jumped bail and ran. Tracked him to Earth, but he's been passing as a native."

"As a *human being?*" Alyson cried.

"As a cat. It's George. Cute li'l George, soft and lazy, lies in the sun all day. Irresponsible behavior. Antisocial. Never gets anything done. Got to bring him back, put him in a work camp."

"Wait a minute," Freddie broke in. "You mean you came to Earth to find an escaped prisoner? And George is it? You mean you're a *cop?*"

"Peace officer," Gilgamesh protested, trying to sit up straight. "Law and order. Loyalty to the egg and arisian pie. Only George *did* escape, so I had to track him down. I always get my amoeba."

Alyson's brother dazedly punched his intercom button. "Miss Blanchard, you'd better cancel the rest of my appointments," he said dully.

"But you *can't* take George away from me!" Alyson cried. "He's my *cat!*"

"Just a third-class amoeba," Gilgamesh sniffed. "Hard to control, though. More trouble than he's worth."

"Then leave him here!" Alyson said. "If he's a fugitive, he's safe with me! I'll give him sanctuary. I'll sign parole papers for him. I'll be responsible—"

Gilgamesh eyed her blearily. "Do you know what you're saying, lady?"

"Of course I know what I'm saying! George is my cat, and I love him—I guess you wouldn't know what that means. George stays with me, no matter what. You go away. Go back to your star."

"Listen, Alyson, maybe you should think about this . . ." Freddie began.

"Shaddup, kid," said Gilgamesh. "I'll tell you, George was never anything to us but a headache. Won't work, just wants to lie around looking decorative. If you want him, lady, you got him."

There was a silence. Freddie noticed that Alyson's brother seemed to be giggling softly to himself.

After long moments, Alyson asked, "Don't I have to sign something?"

"Nah, lady," said Gilgamesh. "We're not barbarians. I've got your voice recorded in my head. George is all yours, and good riddance. He was a blot on the proud record of the Procyon Co-Prosperity Sphere." Gilgamesh got to his feet and marched rigidly to the window of the office. He turned and eyed them greenly.

"Listen, you tell George one thing for me. Tell him he's dumb lucky he happened to hide out as a cat. He can be lazy and decorative here, but I just want you to know one thing: there's no such thing as a decorative amoeba. An amoeba works, or out he goes!"

Gilgamesh disappeared out the window.

On the way back to Alyson's house, Freddie did his best to contain himself, but as they approached her door, he broke their silence. "I told you so, Alyson."

"Told me what?" Alyson opened the door and led him up the stairs to her room.

"That the cat was an alien. A shape-changer, a spy hiding out here on Earth."

"Pooh," she said. "You thought he was from Arcturus. Do you know how far Arcturus is from Procyon?"

They went into her room. "Very far?" Freddie asked.

"Oh, *boy!*" Alyson said. "Very *far!*" She shook her head disgustedly.

George was lying in the middle of the bed, surrounded by schoolbooks. He opened one eye as the two of them tramped into the room, then closed it again and contented himself with a soft purr.

Alyson sat on the side of the bed and rubbed George's belly. "Sweet George," she said. "Beautiful little pussycat."

"Listen, Alyson," said Freddie, "maybe you ought to think about George a little bit. I mean, you're responsible for him now—"

"He's my cat," Alyson said firmly.

"Yeah, well, sort of," Freddie said. "Not really, of course, because really he's an alien shape-changing amoeba from Procyon. And worse than that, remember what Gilgamesh said, he's a runaway. He's a dropout from interstellar society. Who knows, maybe he even uses drugs!"

Alyson rested a level gaze on Freddie, a patient, forgiving look. "Freddie," she said softly, "some of us are born cats, and some of us achieve catness."

"What?"

"Well, look, if *you* were an amoeba from Procyon and you went sent off to the work camps, wouldn't you rather come to Earth and be a cat and lie around all day sunning yourself and getting scratched behind the ears? I mean, it just makes *sense*. It proves George is *sane!*"

"It proves he's lazy," Freddie muttered.

George opened his eyes just a slit and looked at Freddie—a look of contented wonder. Then he closed his eyes again and began to purr.

FULL SUN

Brian W. Aldiss

One of the creatures that has long lurked in the shadows beyond our scientific knowledge is the werewolf, that supernaturally powerful blend of human and animal. Of course, we know werewolves are only a superstition, they're nothing to worry about . . . but maybe that's what they want us to think, so that, unmolested, they may grow in numbers till sometime in the future they can rise again. Here is a story about such a future.

Brian W. Aldiss is the award-winning author of such books as The Long Afternoon of Earth, *and he has recently published a critical history of science fiction,* Billion Year Spree.

The shadows of the endless trees lengthened toward evening and then disappeared, as the sun was consumed by a great pile of cloud on the horizon. Balank was ill at ease, taking his laser rifle from the trundler and tucking it under his arm, although it meant more weight to carry uphill and he was tiring.

The trundler never tired. They had been climbing these hills most of the day, as Balank's thigh muscles informed him, and he had been bent almost double under the oak trees, with the machine always matching his pace beside him, keeping up the hunt.

During much of the wearying day, their instruments told

them that the werewolf was fairly close. Balank remained alert, suspicious of every tree. In the last half hour, though, the scent had faded. When they reached the top of this hill, they would rest—or the man would. The clearing at the top was near now. Under Balank's boots, the layer of dead leaves was thinning.

He had spent too long with his head bent toward the brown-gold carpet; even his retinas were tired. Now he stopped, breathing the sharp air deeply, and stared about. The view behind them, across tumbled and almost un-inhabited country, was magnificent, but Balank gave it scarcely a glance. The infrared warning on the trundler sounded, and the machine pointed a slender rod at a man-sized heat source ahead of them. Balank saw the man almost at the same moment as the machine.

The stranger was standing half concealed behind the trunk of a tree, gazing uncertainly at the trundler and Balank. When Balank raised a hand in tentative greeting, the stranger responded hesitantly. When Balank called out his identification number, the man came cautiously into the open, replying with his own number. The trundler searched in its files, issued an okay, and they moved forward.

As they got level with the man, they saw he had a small mobile hut pitched behind him. He shook hands with Balank, exchanging personal signals, and gave his name as Cyfal.

Balank was a tall, slender man, almost hairless, with the closed expression on his face that might be regarded as characteristic of his epoch. Cyfal, on the other hand, was as slender but much shorter, so that he appeared stockier; his thatch of hair covered all his skull and obtruded slightly onto his face. Something in his manner, or perhaps the expression around his eyes, spoke of the rare type of man whose existence was chiefly spent outside the city.

"I am the timber officer for this region," he said, and indicated his wristcaster as he added, "I was notified you might be in this area, Balank."

"Then you'll know I'm after the werewolf."

"*The* werewolf? There are plenty of them moving through this region, now that the human population is concentrated almost entirely in the cities."

Something in the tone of the remark sounded like social criticism to Balank; he glanced at the trundler without replying.

"Anyhow, you've got a good night to go hunting him," Cyfal said.

"How do you mean?"

"Full moon."

Balank gave no answer. He knew better than Cyfal, he thought, that when the moon was at full, the werewolves reached their time of greatest power.

The trundler was ranging about nearby, an antenna slowly spinning. It made Balank uneasy. He followed it. Man and machine stood together on the edge of a little cliff behind the mobile hut. The cliff was like the curl of foam on the peak of a giant Pacific comber, for here the great wave of earth that was this hill reached its highest point. Beyond, in broken magnificence, it fell down into fresh valleys. The way down was clothed in beeches, just as the way up had been in oaks.

"That's the valley of the Pracha. You can't see the river from here." Cyfal had come up behind them.

"Have you seen anyone who might have been the were-wolf? His real name is Gondalug, identity number YB5921 stroke AS25061, City Zagrad."

Cyfal said, "I saw someone this way this morning. There was more than one of them, I believe." Something in his manner made Balank look at him closely. "I didn't speak to any of them, nor them to me."

"You know them?"

"I've spoken to many men out here in the silent forests,

and found out later they were werewolves. They never harmed me."

Balank said, "But you're afraid of them?"

The half-question broke down Cyfal's reserve. "Of course I'm afraid of them. They're not human—not real men. They're enemies of men. They are, aren't they? They have powers greater than ours."

"They can be killed. They haven't machines, as we have. They're not a serious menace."

"You talk like a city man! How long have you been hunting after this one?"

"Eight days. I had a shot at him once with the laser, but he was gone. He's a gray man, very hairy, sharp features."

"You'll stay and have supper with me? Please. I need someone to talk to."

For supper, Cyfal ate part of a dead wild animal he had cooked. Privately revolted, Balank ate his own rations out of the trundler. In this and other ways, Cyfal was an anachronism. Hardly any timber was needed nowadays in the cities, or had been for millions of years. There remained some marginal uses for wood, necessitating a handful of timber officers, whose main job was to fix signals on old trees that had fallen dangerously, so that machines could fly over later and extract them like rotten teeth from the jaws of the forest. The post of timber officer was being filled more and more by machines, as fewer men were to be found each generation who would take on such a dangerous and lonely job far from the cities.

Over the eons of recorded history, mankind had raised machines that made his cities places of delight. Machines had replaced man's early inefficient machines; machines had replanned forms of transport; machines had come to replan man's life for him. The old stone jungles of man's brief adolescence were buried as deep in memory as the coal jungles of the Carboniferous.

Far away in the pile of discarded yesterdays, man and machines had found how to create life. New foods were produced, neither meat nor vegetable, and the ancient wheel of the past was broken forever, for now the link between man and the land was severed: agriculture, the task of Adam, was as dead as steamships.

Mental attitudes were molded by physical change. As the cities became self-supporting, so mankind needed only cities and the resources of cities. Communications between city and city became so good that physical travel was no longer necessary; city was separated from city by unchecked vegetation as surely as planet is cut off from planet. Few of the hairless denizens of the cities ever thought of outside; those who went physically outside invariably had some element of the abnormal in them.

"The werewolves grow up in cities as we do," Balank said. "It's only in adolescence they break away and seek the wilds. You knew that, I suppose?"

Cyfal's overhead light was unsteady, flickering in an irritating way. "Let's not talk of werewolves after sunset," he said.

"The machines will hunt them all down in time."

"Don't be so sure of that. They're worse at detecting a werewolf than a man is."

"I suppose you realize that's social criticism, Cyfal?"

Cyfal pulled a long sour face and discourteously switched on his wristphone. After a moment, Balank did the same. The operator came up at once, and he asked to be switched to the news satellite.

He wanted to see something fresh on the current time exploration project, but there was nothing new on the files. He was advised to dial back in an hour. Looking over at Cyfal, he saw the timber officer had turned to a dance show of some sort; the cavorting figures in the little projection were badly distorted from this angle. He rose and went to the door of the hut.

The trundler stood outside, ever alert, ignoring him. An untrustworthy light lay over the clearing. Deep twilight reigned, shot through by the rays of the newly risen moon; he was surprised how fast the day had drained away.

Suddenly, he was conscious of himself as an entity, living, with a limited span of life, much of which had already drained away unregarded. The moment of introspection was so uncharacteristic of him that he was frightened. He told himself it was high time he traced down the werewolf and got back to the city: too much solitude was making him morbid.

As he stood there, he heard Cyfal come up behind. The man said, "I'm sorry if I was surly when I was so genuinely glad to see you. It's just that I'm not used to the way city people think. You mustn't take offense—I'm afraid you might even think I'm a werewolf myself."

"That's foolish! We took a blood spec on you as soon as you were within sighting distance." For all that, he realized that Cyfal made him uneasy. Going to where the trundler guarded the door, he took up his laser gun and slipped it under his arm. "Just in case," he said.

"Of course. You think he's around—Gondalug, the werewolf? Maybe following you instead of you following him?"

"As you said, it's full moon. Besides, he hasn't eaten in days. They won't touch synthfoods once the lycanthropic gene asserts itself, you know."

"That's why they eat humans occasionally?" Cyfal stood silent for a moment, then added, "But they are a part of the human race—that is, if you regard them as men who change into wolves rather than wolves who change into men. I mean, they're nearer relations to us than animals or machines are."

"Not than machines!" Balank said in a shocked voice. "How could we survive without the machines?"

Ignoring that, Cyfal said, "To my mind, humans are turning into machines. Myself, I'd rather turn into a werewolf."

Somewhere in the trees, a cry of pain sounded and was repeated.

"Night owl," Cyfal said. The sound brought him back to the present, and he begged Balank to come in and shut the door. He brought out some wine, which they warmed, salted, and drank together.

"The sun's my clock," he said, when they had been chatting for a while. "I shall turn in soon. You'll sleep too?"

"I don't sleep—I've a fresher."

"I never had the operation. Are you moving on? Look, are you planning to leave me here all alone, the night of the full moon?" He grabbed Balank's sleeve and then withdrew his hand.

"If Gondalug's about, I want to kill him tonight. I must get back to the city." But he saw that Cyfal was frightened and took pity on the little man. "But in fact I could manage an hour's freshing—I've had none for three days."

"You'll take it here?"

"Sure, get your head down—but you're armed, aren't you?"

"It doesn't always do you any good."

While the little man prepared his bunk, Balank switched on his phone again. The news feature was ready and came up almost at once. Again Balank was plunged into a remote and terrible future.

The machines had managed to push their time exploration some eight million million years ahead, and there a deviation in the quanta of the electromagnetic spectrum had halted their advance. The reason for this was so far obscure and lay in the changing nature of the sun, which strongly influenced the time structure of its own minute corner of the galaxy.

Balank was curious to find if the machines had resolved the problem. It appeared that they had not, for the main news of the day was that Platform One had decided that operations should now be confined to the span of time already opened up. Platform One was the name of the machine civilization, many hundreds of centuries ahead in time, which had first pushed through the time barrier and contacted all machine-ruled civilizations before its own epoch.

What a disappointment that only the electronic senses of machines could shuttle in time! Balank would greatly have liked to visit one of the great cities of the remote future.

The compensation was that the explorers sent back video pictures of that world to their own day. These alien landscapes produced in Balank a tremendous hunger for more; he looked in whenever he could. Even on the trail of the werewolf, which absorbed almost all his faculties, he had dialed for every possible picture of that inaccessible and terrific reality that lay distantly on the same time stratum which contained his own world.

As the first transmissions took on cubic content, Balank heard a noise outside the hut, and was instantly on his feet. Grabbing the gun, he opened the door and peered out, his left hand on the doorjamb, his wristset still working.

The trundler sat outside, its senses ever functioning, fixing him with an indicator as if in unfriendly greeting. A leaf or two drifted down from the trees; it was never absolutely silent here, as it could be in the cities at night; there was always something living or dying in the unmapped woods. As he turned his gaze through the darkness—but of course the trundler—and the werewolf, it was said—saw much more clearly in this situation than he did—his vision was obscured by the representation of the future palely gleaming at his cuff. Two phases of the same world were in juxtaposition, one standing on its side, promising an environment where different senses would be needed to survive.

Satisfied, although still wary, Balank shut the door and went to sit down and study the transmission. When it was over, he dialed a repeat. Catching his absorption, Cyfal from his bunk dialed the same program.

Above the icy deserts of Earth a blue sun shone, too small

to show a disk, and from this chip of light came all terrestrial change. Its light was bright as full moon's light, and scarcely warmer. Only a few strange and stunted types of vegetation stretched up from the mountains toward it. All the old primitive kinds of flora had vanished long ago. Trees, for so many epochs one of the sovereign forms of Earth, had gone. Animals had gone. Birds had vanished from the skies. In the mountainous seas, very few life-forms protracted their existence.

New forces had inherited this later Earth. This was the time of the majestic auroras, of the near absolute-zero nights, of the years-long blizzards.

But there were cities still, their lights burning brighter than the chilly sun; and there were the machines.

The machines of this distant age were monstrous and complex things, slow and armored, resembling most the dinosaurs that had filled one hour of the Earth's dawn. They foraged over the bleak landscape on their own ineluctable errands. They climbed into space, building their monstrous webbed arms that stretched far from Earth's orbit, to scoop in energy and confront the poor fish sun with a vast trawler net of magnetic force.

In the natural course of its evolution, the sun had developed into its white dwarf stage. Its phase as a yellow star, when it supported vertebrate life, was a brief one, now passed through. Now it moved toward its prime season, still far ahead, when it would enter the main period of its life and become a red dwarf star. Then it would be mature, then it would itself be invested with an awareness countless times greater than any minor consciousness it nourished now. As the machines clad in their horned exoskeletons climbed near it, the sun had entered a period of quiescence to be measured in billions of years, and cast over its third planet the light of a perpetual full moon.

The documentary presenting this image of postiquity

carried a commentary that consisted mainly of a rundown of
the technical difficulties confronting Platform One and the
other machine civilizations at that time. It was too complex
for Balank to understand. He looked up from his phone at
last, and saw that Cyfal had dropped asleep in his bunk. By
his wrist, against his tousled head, a shrunken sun still
burned.

For some moments, Balank stood looking speculatively at
the timber officer. The man's criticism of the machines disturbed him. Naturally, people were always criticizing the machines, but, after all, mankind depended on them more and
more, and most of the criticism was superficial. Cyfal seemed
to doubt the whole role of machines.

It was extremely difficult to decide just how much truth lay
in anything. The werewolves, for example. They were and always had been man's enemy, and that was presumably why
the machines hunted them with such ruthlessness—for man's
sake. But from what he had learned at the patrol school, the
creatures were on the increase. And had they really got magic
powers? Powers, that was to say, that were beyond man's, that
enabled them to survive and flourish as man could not, even
supported by all the forces of the cities? The Dark Brother:
that was what they called the werewolf, because he was like
the night side of man. But he was not man—and how exactly
he differed, nobody could tell, except that he could survive
when man had not.

Still frowning, Balank moved across to the door and looked
out. The moon was climbing, casting a pallid and dappled
light among the trees of the clearing, and across the trundler.
Balank was reminded of that distant day when the sun would
shine no more warmly.

The trundler was switched to transmission, and Balank
wondered with whom it was in touch. With Headquarters,
possibly, asking for fresh orders, sending in their report.

"I'm taking an hour with my fresher," he said. "Okay by you?"

"Go ahead. I shall stand guard," the trundler's speech circuit said.

Balank went back inside, sat down at the table and clipped the fresher across his forehead. He fell instantly into unconsciousness, an unconsciousness that force-fed him enough sleep and dream to refresh him for the next seventy-two hours. At the end of the timed hour he awoke, annoyingly aware that there had been confusion in his skull.

Before he had lifted his head from the table, the thought came: we never saw any human beings in that chilly future.

He sat up straight. Of course, it had just been an accidental omission from a brief program. Humans were not so important as the machines, and that would apply even more in the distant time. But none of the news flashes had shown humans, not even in the immense cities. That was absurd; there would be lots of human beings. The machines had covenanted, at the time of the historic Emancipation, that they would always protect the human race.

Well, Balank told himself, he was talking nonsense. The subversive comments Cyfal had uttered had put a load of mischief into his head. Instinctively, he glanced over at the timber officer.

Cyfal was dead in his bunk. He lay contorted with his head lolling over the side of the mattress, his throat torn out. Blood still welled up from the wound, dripping very slowly from one shoulder onto the floor.

Forcing himself to do it, Balank went over to him. In one of Cyfal's hands, a piece of gray fur was gripped.

The werewolf had called! Balank gripped his throat in terror. He had evidently roused in time to save his own life, and the creature had fled.

He stood for a long time staring down in pity and horror at the dead man, before prizing the piece of fur from his grasp.

He examined it with distaste. It was softer than he had imagined wolf fur to be. He turned the hairs over in his palm. A piece of skin had torn away with the hair. He looked at it more closely.

A letter was printed on the skin.

It was faint, but he definitely picked out an "S" to one edge of the skin. No, it must be a bruise, a stain, anything but a printed letter. That would mean that this was synthetic, and had been left as a fragment of evidence to mislead Balank. . . .

He ran over to the door, grabbed up the laser gun as he went, and dashed outside. The moon was high now. He saw the trundler moving across the clearing toward him.

"Where have you been?" he called.

"Patrolling. I heard something among the trees and got a glimpse of a large gray wolf, but was not able to destroy it. Why are you frightened? I am registering surplus adrenaline in your veins."

"Come in and look. Something killed the timber man."

He stood aside as the machine entered the hut and extended a couple of rods above the body on the bunk. As he watched, Balank pushed the piece of fur down into his pocket.

"Cyfal is dead. His throat has been ripped out. It is the work of a large animal. Balank, if you are rested, we must now pursue the werewolf Gondalug, identity number YB5921 stroke AS25061. He committed this crime."

They went outside. Balank found himself trembling. He said, "Shouldn't we bury the poor fellow?"

"If necessary, we can return by daylight."

Argument was impossible with trundlers. This one was already off, and Balank was forced to follow.

They moved downhill toward the River Pracha. The difficulty of the descent soon drove everything else from Balank's mind. They had followed Gondalug this far, and it

seemed unlikely he would go much farther. Beyond here lay
gaunt, bleak uplands, lacking cover. In this broken, tumbling
valley, Gondalug would go to earth, hoping to hide from
them. But their instruments would track him down, and then
he could be destroyed. With good luck, he would lead them
to caves where they would find and exterminate other men
and women and maybe children who bore the deadly
lycanthropic gene and refused to live in cities.

It took them two hours to get down to the lower part of the
valley. Great slabs of the hill had fallen away and now stood
apart from their parent body, forming cubic hills in their own
right, with great sandy cliffs towering up vertically, crowned
with unruly foliage. The Pracha itself frequently disappeared
down narrow crevices, and the whole area was broken with
caves and fissures in the rock. It was ideal country in which to
hide.

"I must rest for a moment," Balank gasped. The trundler
came immediately to a halt. It moved over any terrain, putting out short legs to help itself when tracks and wheels
failed.

They stood together, ill-assorted in the pale night, surrounded by the noise of the little river as it battled over its
rocky bed.

"You're sending again, aren't you? Whom to?"

The machine asked, "Why did you conceal the piece of
wolf fur you found in the timber officer's hand?"

Balank was running at once, diving for cover behind the
nearest slab of rock. Sprawling in the dirt, he saw a beam of
heat sizzle above him and slewed himself around the corner.
The Pracha ran along here in a steep-sided crevasse. With
fear lending him strength Balank took a run and cleared the
crevasse in a mighty jump and fell among the shadows on the
far side of the gulf. He crawled behind a great chunk of rock,
the flat top of which was several feet above his head, crowned
with a sagging pine tree.

The trundler called to him from the other side of the river. "Balank, Balank, you have gone wrong in your head!"

Staying firmly behind the rock, he shouted back, "Go home, trundler! You'll never find me here!"

"Why did you conceal the piece of wolf fur from the timber officer's hand?"

"How did you know about the fur unless you put it there? You killed Cyfal because he knew things about machines I did not, didn't you? You wanted me to believe the werewolf did it, didn't you? The machines are gradually killing off the humans, aren't they? There are no such things as werewolves, are there?"

"You are mistaken, Balank. There are werewolves, all right. Because man would never really believe they existed, they have survived. But we believe they exist, and to us they are a greater menace than mankind can be now. So surrender and come back to me. We will continue looking for Gondalug."

He did not answer. He crouched and listened to the machine prowling on the other side of the river.

Crouching on top of the rock above Balank's head was a sinewy man with a flat skull. He took more than human advantage of every shade of cover as he drank in the scene below, his brain running through the possibilities of the situation as efficiently as his legs could take him through wild grass. He waited without stirring, and his face was gray and grave and alert.

The machine came to a decision. Getting no reply from the man, it came gingerly around the rock and approached the edge of the crevasse through which the river ran. Experimentally, it sent a blast of heat across to the opposite cliff, followed by a brief hail of armored pellets.

"Balank?" it called.

Balank did not reply, but the trundler was convinced it had not killed the man. It had somehow to get across the brink

Balank had jumped. It considered radioing for aid, but the nearest city, Zagrad, was a great distance away.

It stretched out its legs, extending them as far as possible. Its clawed feet could just reach the other side, but there the edge crumbled slightly and would not support its full weight. It shuffled slowly along the crevasse, seeking out the ideal place.

From shelter, Balank watched it glinting with a murderous dullness in the moonlight. He clutched a great shard of rock, knowing what he had to do. He had presented to him here the best—probably the only—chance he would get to destroy the machine. When it was hanging across the ravine, he would rush forward. The trundler would be momentarily too preoccupied to burn him down. He would hurl the boulder at it, knock the vile thing down into the river.

The machine was quick and clever. He would have only a split second in which to act. Already his muscles bulged over the rock, already he gritted his teeth in effort, already his eyes glared ahead at the hated enemy. His time would come at any second now. It was him or it. . . .

Gondalug alertly stared down at the scene, involved with it and yet detached. He saw what was in the man's mind, knew that he looked a scant second ahead to the encounter.

His own kind, man's Dark Brother, worked differently. They looked farther ahead, just as they had always done, in a fashion unimaginable to Homo sapiens. To Gondalug, the outcome of this particular little struggle was immaterial. He knew that his kind had already won their battle against mankind. He knew that they still had to enter into their real battle against the machines.

But that time would come. And then they would defeat the machines. In the long days when the sun shone always over the blessed Earth like a full moon—in those days, his kind would finish their age of waiting and enter into their own savage kingdom.

THE SILENT COLONY

Robert Silverberg

If explorers from a distant planet were to visit Earth, our world would seem terribly strange to them, full of strange colors and smells and feelings. And even if they found something familiar, that too could pose a sudden deadly danger.

Robert Silverberg is one of the premier writers of modern science fiction. His most recent novel is The Stochastic Man.

Skrid, Emerak, and Ullowa drifted through the dark night of space, searching the worlds that passed below them for some sign of their own kind. The urge to wander had come over them, as it does inevitably to all inhabitants of the Ninth World. They had been drifting through space for eons; but time is no barrier to immortals, and they were patient searchers.

"I think I feel something," said Emerak; "the Third World is giving off signs of life."

They had visited the thriving cities of the Eighth World, and the struggling colonies of the Seventh, and the experienced Skrid had led them to the little-known settlements on the moons of the giant Fifth World. But now they were far from home.

"You're mistaken, youngster," said Skrid. "There can't be any life on a planet so close to the sun as the Third World—think of how warm it is!"

Emerak turned bright white with rage. "Can't you *feel* the life down there? It's not much, but it's there. Maybe you're too old, Skrid."

Skrid ignored the insult. "I think we should turn back; we're putting ourselves in danger by going so close to the sun. We've seen enough."

"No, Skrid, I detect life below." Emerak blazed angrily. "And just because you're leader of this triad doesn't mean that you know everything. It's just that your form is more complex than ours, and it'll only be a matter of time until—"

"Quiet, Emerak." It was the calm voice of Ullowa. "Skrid, I think the hothead's right. I'm picking up weak impressions from the Third World myself; there may be some primitive life-forms evolving there. We'll never forgive ourselves if we turn back now."

"But the sun, Ullowa, the sun! If we go too close—" Skrid was silent, and the three drifted on through the void. After a while he said, "All right, let's investigate."

The three accordingly changed their direction and began to head for the Third World. They spiraled slowly down through space until the planet hung before them, a mottled bowl spinning endlessly.

Invisibly they slipped down and into its atmosphere, gently drifting toward the planet below. They strained to pick up signs of life, and as they approached the life-impulses grew stronger. Emerak cried out vindictively that Skrid should listen to him more often. They knew now, without doubt, that their kind of life inhabited the planet.

"Hear that, Skrid? Listen to it, old one."

"All right, Emerak," the elder being said, "you've proved your point. I never claimed to be infallible."

"These are pretty strange thought-impressions coming up, Skrid. Listen to them, they have no minds down there," said Ullowa. "They don't think."

"Fine," exulted Skrid. "We can teach them the ways of

civilization and raise them to our level. It shouldn't be hard, when time is ours."

"Yes," Ullowa agreed, "they're so mindless that they'll be putty in our hands. Skrid's Colony, we'll call the planet. I can just see the way the Council will go for this. A new colony, discovered by the noted adventurer Skrid and two fearless companions—"

"Skrid's Colony, I like the sound of that," said Skrid. "Look, there's a drifting colony of them now, falling to earth. Let's join them and make contact; here's our chance to begin."

They entered the colony and drifted slowly to the ground among them. Skrid selected a place where a heap of them lay massed together, and made a skilled landing, touching all six of his delicately constructed limbs to the ground and sinking almost thankfully into a position of repose. Ullowa and Emerak followed and landed nearby.

"I can't detect any minds among them," complained Emerak, frantically searching through the beings near him. "They look just like us—that is, as close a resemblance as is possible for one of us to have to another. But they don't think."

Skrid sent a prying beam of thought into the heap on which he was lying. He entered first one, then another, of the inhabitants.

"Very strange," he reported. "I think they've just been born; many of them have vague memories of the liquid state, and some can recall as far back as the vapor state. I think we've stumbled over something important, thanks to Emerak."

"This is wonderful!" Ullowa said. "Here's our opportunity to study newborn entities firsthand."

"It's a relief to find some people younger than yourself," Emerak said sardonically. "I'm so used to being the baby of the group that it feels peculiar to have all these infants around."

"It's quite glorious," Ullowa said, as he propelled himself over the ground to where Skrid was examining one of the beings. "It hasn't been for a million ten-years that a newborn has appeared on our world, and here we are with billions of them all around."

"Two million ten-years, Ullowa," Skrid corrected. "Emerak here is of the last generation. And no need for any more, either, not while the mature entities live forever, barring accidents. But this is a big chance for us—we can make a careful study of these newborn ones, and perhaps set up a rudimentary culture here, and report to the Council once these babies have learned to govern themselves. We can start completely from scratch on the Third Planet. This discovery will rank with Kodranik's vapor theory!"

"I'm glad you allowed me to come," said Emerak. "It isn't often that a youngster like me gets a chance to—" Emerak's voice tailed off in a cry of amazement and pain.

"Emerak?" questioned Skrid. There was no reply.

"Where did the youngster go? What happened?" Ullowa said.

"Some fool stunt, I suppose. That little speech of his was too good to be true, Ullowa."

"No, I can't seem to locate him anywhere. Can you? Uh, Skrid! Help me! I'm—I'm—Skrid, it's killing me!"

The sense of pain that burst from Ullowa was very real, and it left Skrid trembling. "Ullowa! Ullowa!"

Skrid felt fear for the first time in more eons than he could remember, and the unfamiliar fright-sensation disturbed his sensitively balanced mind. "Emerak! Ullowa! Why don't you answer?"

Is this the end, Skrid thought, the end of everything? Are we going to perish here after so many years of life? To die alone and unattended, on a dismal planet billions of miles from home? Death was a concept too alien for him to accept.

He called again, his impulses stronger this time. "Emerak! Ullowa! Where are you?"

In panic, he shot beams of thought all around, but the only radiations he picked up were the mindless ones of the newly born.

"Ullowa!"

There was no answer, and Skrid began to feel his fragile body disintegrating. The limbs he had been so proud of—so complex and finely traced—began to blur and twist. He sent out one more frantic cry, feeling the weight of his great age, and sensing the dying thoughts of the newly born around him. Then he melted and trickled away over the heap, while the newborn snowflakes of the Third World watched uncomprehending, even as their own doom was upon them. The sun was beginning to climb over the horizon, and its deadly warmth beat down.

THE STREET
THAT WASN'T THERE

Clifford D. Simak
and Carl Jacobi

Many science fiction writers have theorized that there might be other "dimensions" or other "planes" of reality, inhabited by beings totally unknown to us. But what if such eerie creatures began to make their way into our world? What effect would they have on us? This deceptively quiet story suggests an unexpected kind of invasion from beyond.

Both Clifford Simak and Carl Jacobi are long-time authors of science fiction, their earliest stories dating back into the 1930's. The Street That Wasn't There, written when they were both members of the Minneapolis Fantasy Society, is their only collaboration.

Mr. Jonathan Chambers left his house on Maple Street at exactly seven o'clock in the evening and set out on the daily walk he had taken, at the same time, come rain or snow, for twenty solid years.

The walk never varied. He paced two blocks down Maple Street, stopped at the Red Star confectionery to buy a Rosa Trofero perfecto, then walked to the end of the fourth block on Maple. There he turned right on Lexington, followed Lexington to Oak, down Oak and so by way of Lincoln back to Maple again and to his home.

He took his time. He always returned to his front door at exactly seven forty-five. No one ever stopped to talk with him. Even the man at the Red Star confectionery, where he bought his cigar, remained silent while the purchase was being made. Mr. Chambers merely tapped on the glass top of the counter with a coin, the man reached in and brought forth the box, and Mr. Chambers took his cigar. That was all.

For people long ago had gathered that Mr. Chambers desired to be left alone. The newer generation of townsfolk called it eccentricity. Certain uncouth persons had a different word for it. The oldsters remembered that this queer-looking individual with his black silk muffler, rosewood cane, and bowler hat once had been a professor at State University.

A professor of metaphysics, they seemed to recall, or some such outlandish subject. At any rate, a furore of some sort was connected with his name—at the time an academic scandal. He had written a book, and he had taught the subject matter of that volume to his classes. What that subject matter was had been long forgotten, but it had been considered sufficiently revolutionary to cost Mr. Chambers his post at the University.

A silver moon shone over the chimneytops and a chill, impish October wind was rustling the dead leaves when Mr. Chambers started out at seven o'clock. It was a good night, he told himself, smelling the clean, crisp air of autumn and the faint pungence of distant wood smoke.

He walked unhurriedly, swinging his cane a bit less jauntily than twenty years ago. He tucked the muffler more securely under the rusty old topcoat and pulled his bowler hat more firmly on his head. He noticed that the streetlight at the corner of Maple and Jefferson was out, and he grumbled a little to himself when he was forced to step off the walk to encircle a boarded-off section of newly laid concrete work before the driveway of 816.

It seemed that he reached the corner of Lexington and

Maple just a bit too quickly, but he told himself that this couldn't be. For he had never done that. For twenty years, since the year following his expulsion from the University, he had lived by the clock. The same thing, at the same time, day after day. He had not deliberately set upon such a life of routine. A bachelor, living alone with sufficient money to supply his humble needs, the timed existence had grown on him gradually.

So he turned on Lexington and back on Oak. The dog at the corner of Oak and Jefferson was waiting for him once again and came out snarling and growling, snapping at his heels. But Mr. Chambers pretended not to notice and the beast gave up the chase.

A radio blared down the street and faint phrases floated to Mr. Chambers.

". . . still taking place . . . Empire State building disappeared . . . thin air . . . famed scientist, Dr. Edmund Harcourt . . ."

The wind whipped the muted words away and Mr. Chambers grumbled to himself. Another one of those fantastic radio dramas, probably. He remembered one from many years before, something about the Martians. And Harcourt! What did Harcourt have to do with it? He was one of the men who had ridiculed the book Mr. Chambers had written.

But he pushed speculation away, sniffed the clean, crisp air again, looked at the familiar things that materialized out of the late-autumn darkness as he walked along. For there was nothing, absolutely nothing in the world, that he would let upset him. That was a tenet he had laid down twenty years ago.

There was a crowd of men talking excitedly in front of the drugstore at the corner of Oak and Lincoln. Mr. Chambers caught sentences: "It's happening everywhere. . . . What do you think it is? . . . The scientists can't explain . . ."

But as Mr. Chambers neared them they fell into what

seemed an abashed silence and watched him pass. He, on his part, gave them no sign of recognition. That was the way it had been for many years, ever since the people had become convinced that he did not wish to talk. One of the men half started forward as if to speak to him, but then stepped back and Mr. Chambers continued on his walk.

Back at his own front door he stopped and, as he had done a thousand times before, drew forth the heavy gold watch from his pocket.

He started violently. It was only seven-thirty!

For long minutes he stood there staring at the watch in accusation. The timepiece had not stopped, for it still ticked audibly. But fifteen minutes too soon! For twenty years, day in, day out, he had started out at seven and returned at quarter to eight.

It was not until then that he realized something else was wrong. He had no cigar. For the first time he had neglected to purchase his evening smoke.

Shaken, muttering to himself, Mr. Chambers let himself into his house and locked the door behind him. He hung his hat and coat on the rack in the hall and walked into the living room. Dropping into his favorite chair, he shook his head in bewilderment.

Silence filled the room, a silence measured by the ticking of the old-fashioned pendulum clock on the mantelpiece. But silence was no strange thing to Mr. Chambers. Once he had loved music, the kind of music he could get by tuning in symphonic orchestras on the radio. But the radio stood silent in the corner, the cord out of its socket. Mr. Chambers had pulled it out many years before, on the night when the symphonic broadcast had been interrupted to give a news flash.

He had stopped reading newspapers and magazines, too, had exiled himself to a few city blocks. And as the years flowed by, that self-exile had become a prison, an intangible, impassable wall bounded by four city blocks by three. Beyond them lay utter, unexplainable terror. Beyond them he never went.

But recluse though he was, he could not on occasion escape from hearing things the newsboy shouted on the street, things the men talked about on the drugstore corner when they failed to see him coming. And so he knew that this was the year 1960 and that the war in Europe and Asia had flamed to an end to be followed by a terrible plague, a plague that even now was sweeping through country after country like a wildfire, decimating populations, a plague undoubtedly induced by hunger and privation and the miseries of war.

Those things he put away as items far removed from his own small world. He disregarded them. He pretended he had never heard of them. Others might discuss and worry over them if they wished. To him they simply did not matter. But there were two things tonight that did matter. Two curious, incredible events. He had arrived home fifteen minutes early. He had forgotten his cigar.

Huddled in the chair, he frowned slowly. It was disquieting to have something like that happen. There must be something wrong. Had his long exile finally turned his mind—perhaps just a very little—enough to make him queer? Had he lost his sense of proportion, of perspective?

No, he had not. Take this room, for example. After twenty years it had come to be as much a part of him as the clothes he wore. Every detail of the room was engraved in his mind with clarity: the old center leg table with its green covering and stained-glass lamp; the mantelpiece with the dusty bric-a-brac; the pendulum clock that told the time of day as well as the day of the week and month; the elephant ash tray on the tabaret and, most important of all, the marine print.

Mr. Chambers loved that picture. It had depth, he always said. It showed an old sailing ship in the foreground on a placid sea. Far in the distance, almost on the horizon line, was the vague outline of a larger vessel. There were other pictures, too. The forest scene above the fireplace, the old English prints in the corner where he sat, the Currier and Ives above the radio. But the ship print was directly in his line of vision. He could see it without turning his head. He had put it there because he liked it best.

Further reverie became an effort as Mr. Chambers felt himself succumbing to weariness. He undressed and went to bed. For an hour he lay awake, assailed by vague fears he could neither define nor understand.

When finally he dozed off it was to lose himself in a series of horrific dreams. He dreamed first that he was a castaway on a tiny islet in mid-ocean, that the waters around the island teemed with huge poisonous sea snakes, hydrophinnae, and that steadily those serpents were devouring the island.

In another dream he was pursued by a horror that he could neither see nor hear, but only could imagine. And as he sought to flee he stayed in the one place. His legs worked frantically, pumping like pistons, but he could make no progress. It was as if he ran upon a treadway.

Then again the terror descended on him, a black, unimagined thing, and he tried to scream and could not. He opened his mouth and strained his vocal cords and filled his lungs to bursting with the urge to shriek, but not a sound came from his lips.

All next day he was uneasy and, as he left the house that evening at precisely seven o'clock, he kept saying to himself: "I must not forget tonight! I must remember to stop and get my cigar!"

The streetlight at the corner of Jefferson was still out and in front of 816 the cemented driveway was still boarded off. Everything was the same as the night before. And now, he told himself, the Red Star confectionery is in the next block. I must not forget tonight. To forget twice in a row would be just too much. He grasped that thought firmly in his mind, strode just a bit more rapidly down the street.

But at the corner he stopped in consternation, and stared down the next block. There was no neon sign, no splash of friendly light upon the sidewalk to mark the little store tucked away in this residential section.

He stared at the street marker and read the word slowly: GRANT. He read it again, unbelieving, for this should not be Grant Street, but Marshall. He had walked two blocks and the confectionery was between Marshall and Grant. He hadn't come to Marshall yet—and here was Grant.

Or had he, absentmindedly, come one block farther than he thought, passed the store as on the night before?

For the first time in twenty years, Mr. Chambers retraced his steps. He walked back to Jefferson, then turned around and went back to Grant again and on to Lexington. Then back to Grant again, where he stood astounded while a single, incredible fact grew slowly in his brain:

There was no confectionery! The block from Marshall to Grant had disappeared!

Now he understood why he had missed the store on the night before, why he had arrived home fifteen minutes early.

On shaky legs he stumbled back to his home. He slammed and locked the door behind him and made his way unsteadily to his chair in the corner.

What was this? What did it mean? By what inconceivable necromancy could a paved street with houses, trees, and buildings be spirited away and the space it had occupied be closed up? Was something happening in the world which he, in his secluded life, knew nothing about?

Mr. Chambers shivered, reached to turn up the collar of his coat, then stopped as he realized the room must be warm. A fire blazed merrily in the grate. The cold he felt came from something, somewhere else. The cold of fear and horror, the chill of a half-whispered thought.

A deathly silence had fallen, a silence still measured by the pendulum clock, and yet one that held a different tenor from any he had ever sensed before. Not a homey, comfortable silence—but a silence that hinted at emptiness and nothingness.

There was something back of this, Mr. Chambers told himself. Something that reached far back into one corner of his brain and demanded recognition. Something tied up with the fragments of talk he had heard on the drugstore corner, bits of news broadcasts he had heard as he walked along the street, the shrieking of the newsboy calling his papers. Something to do with the happenings in the world from which he had excluded himself.

He brought them back to mind now and lingered over the one central theme of the talk he overheard: the wars and plagues. Hints of a Europe and Asia swept almost clean of human life, of the plague ravaging Africa, of its appearance in South America, of the frantic efforts of the United States to prevent its spread into that nation's boundaries.

Millions of people were dead in Europe and Asia, Africa and South America. And somehow those gruesome statistics seemed tied up with his own experience. Something, somewhere, some part of his earlier life, seemed to hold an explanation.

The pendulum clock struck slowly, its every other chime as usual setting up a sympathetic vibration in the pewter vase that stood upon the mantel.

Mr. Chambers got to his feet, strode to the door, opened it and looked out. Moonlight tessellated the street in black and silver, etching the chimneys and trees against a silvered sky. But the house directly across the street was not the same. It was strangely lopsided, its dimensions out of proportion, like a house that suddenly had gone mad.

He stared at it in amazement, trying to determine what was

wrong with it. He recalled how it had always stood, four-square, a solid piece of mid-Victorian architecture.

Then, before his eyes, the house righted itself again. Slowly it drew together, ironed out its queer angles, readjusted its dimensions, became once again the stodgy house he knew it had to be.

With a sigh of relief, Mr. Chambers turned back into the hall. But before he closed the door, he looked again. The house was lopsided—as bad as, perhaps worse than before!

Gulping in fright, Mr. Chambers slammed the door shut, locked it and double-bolted it. Then he went to his bedroom and took sleeping powders.

His dreams that night were the same as on the night before. Again there was the islet in mid-ocean. Again he was alone upon it. Again the squirming hydrophinnae were eating his foothold piece by piece.

He awoke, body drenched with perspiration. Vague light of early dawn filtered through the window. The clock on the bedside table showed seven-thirty. For a long time he lay there motionless.

Again the fantastic happenings of the night before came back to haunt him and, as he lay there staring at the windows, he remembered them, one by one. But his mind, still fogged by sleep and astonishment, took the happenings in its stride, mulled over them, lost the keen edge of fantastic terror that lurked around them.

The light through the windows slowly grew brighter. Mr. Chambers slid out of bed and crossed to the window, the cold of the floor biting into his bare feet. He forced himself to look out.

There was nothing outside the window. No shadows. As if there might be a fog. But no fog, however thick, could hide the apple tree that grew close against the house.

But the tree *was* there—shadowy, indistinct in the gray, with a few withered apples still clinging to its boughs, a few

shriveled leaves reluctant to leave the parent branch. The tree
was there now. But it had not been there when he first had
looked. Mr. Chambers was sure of that.

And now he saw the faint outlines of his neighbor's house
—but those outlines were all wrong. They didn't jibe and fit
together, they were out of plumb, as if some giant hand had
grasped the house and wrenched it out of true, like the house
he had seen across the street the night before, the house that
had painfully righted itself when he thought of how it should
look.

Perhaps if he thought of how his neighbor's house should
look, it too might right itself. But Mr. Chambers was very
weary. Too weary to think about the house. He turned from
the window and dressed slowly. In the living room he
slumped into his chair, put his feet on the old cracked ot-
toman. For a long time he sat, trying to think.

And then, abruptly, something like an electric shock ran
through him. Rigid, he sat there, limp inside at the thought.
Minutes later he crossed the room to the old mahogany bookcase that stood against the wall. There were many volumes in
the case: his beloved classics on the first shelf, his many
scientific works on the lower shelves. The second shelf contained but one book around which Mr. Chambers' entire life
was centered.

Twenty years ago he had written it and foolishly attempted
to teach its philosophy to a class of undergraduates. The
newspapers, he remembered, had made a great deal of it at
the time. Tongues had been set to wagging. Narrow-minded
townsfolk failing to understand either his philosophy or his
aim, but seeing in him another exponent of some antirational
cult, had forced his expulsion from the school.

It was a simple book, really, dismissed by most authorities
as merely the vagaries of an overzealous mind. Mr. Chambers
took it down now, opened its cover and began thumbing

through the pages. For a moment the memory of happier days swept over him.

Then his eyes found the paragraph, a paragraph written so long ago that the very words seemed strange and unreal:

Man himself, by the power of mass suggestion, holds the physical fate of this earth, yes, even of the universe. Millions of minds seeing trees as trees, houses as houses, streets as streets, and not as something else. Minds that see things as they are and have kept things as they were. . . . Destroy those minds and the entire foundation of matter, robbed of its regenerative power, will crumple and slip away like a column of sand. . . .

His eyes followed down the page:

Yet this would have nothing to do with matter itself, but only with matter's form. For while the mind of man through long ages may have molded an imagery of that space in which he lives, mind would have little conceivable influence upon the existence of that matter. What exists in our known universe shall exist always and can never be destroyed, only altered or transformed.

But in modern astrophysics and mathematics we gain an insight into the possibility and probability that there are other dimensions, other brackets of time and space impinging on the one we occupy. If a pin is thrust into a shadow, would that shadow have any knowledge of the pin? It would not, for in this case the shadow is two-dimensional, the pin three-dimensional. Yet both occupy the same space.

Granting then that the power of men's minds alone holds this universe, or at least this world in its present form, may we not go farther and envision other minds on some other plane watching us, waiting, waiting craftily for the time they can take over the domination of matter? Such a concept is not impossible. It is a natural conclusion if we accept the double hypothesis: that mind does control the formation of all matter; and that other worlds lie in juxta-position with ours.

Perhaps we shall come upon a day, far distant, when our plane, our world will dissolve beneath our feet and before our eyes as some stronger intelligence reaches out from the dimensional shadows of the very space we live in and wrests from us the matter which we know to be our own.

He stood astounded beside the bookcase, his eyes staring unseeing into the fire upon the hearth. *He* had written that. And because of those words he had been called a heretic, had been compelled to resign his position at the University, had been forced into this hermit life.

A tumultuous idea hammered at him. Men had died by the millions all over the world. Where there had been thousands of minds there now were one or two. A feeble force to hold the form of matter intact. The plague had swept Europe and Asia almost clean of life, had blighted Africa, had reached South America—might even have come to the United States. He remembered the whispers he had heard, the words of the men at the drugstore corner, the buildings disappearing. Something scientists could not explain. But those were merely scraps of information. He did not know the whole story . . . he could not know. He never listened to the radio, never read a newspaper.

But abruptly the whole thing fitted together in his brain like the missing piece of a puzzle into its slot. The significance of it all gripped him with damning clarity. There were not sufficient minds in existence to retain the material world in its mundane form. Some other power from another dimension was fighting to supersede man's control *and take his universe into its own plane!*

Abruptly Mr. Chambers closed the book, shoved it back in

the case and picked up his hat and coat. He had to know more. He had to find someone who could tell him. He moved through the hall to the door, emerged into the street. On the walk he looked skyward, trying to make out the sun. But there was no sun—only an all-pervading grayness that shrouded everything, not a fog, but a gray emptiness that seemed devoid of life, of any movement.

The walk led to his gate and there it ended, but as he moved forward the sidewalk came into view and the house ahead loomed out of the gray, but a house with differences.

He moved forward rapidly. Visibility extended only a few feet, and as he approached them the houses materialized like two-dimensional pictures without perspective, like twisted cardboard soldiers lining up for review on a misty morning. Once he stopped and looked back and saw that the grayness had closed in behind him. The houses were wiped out, the sidewalk faded into nothing.

He shouted, hoping to attract attention. But his voice frightened him. It seemed to ricochet up and into the higher levels of the sky, as if a giant door had been opened to a mighty room high above him.

He went on until he came to the corner of Lexington. There, on the curb, he stopped and stared. The gray wall was thicker there but he did not realize how close it was until he glanced down at his feet and saw there was nothing, nothing at all beyond the curbstone. No dull gleam of wet asphalt, no sign of a street. It was as if all eternity ended here at the corner of Maple and Lexington.

With a wild cry, Mr. Chambers turned and ran. Back down the street he raced, coat streaming after him in the wind, bowler hat bouncing on his head.

Panting, he reached the gate and stumbled up the walk, thankful that it still was there.

On the stoop he stood for a moment, breathing hard. He glanced back over his shoulder and a queer feeling of inner numbness seemed to well over him. At that moment the gray nothingness appeared to thin, the enveloping curtain fell away, and he saw . . .

Vague and indistinct, yet cast in stereoscopic outline, a gigantic city was limned against the darkling sky. It was a city fantastic with cubed domes, spires, and aerial bridges and flying buttresses. Tunnel-like streets, flanked on either side by shining metallic ramps and runways, stretched endlessly to the vanishing point. Great shafts of multicolored light probed huge streamers and ellipses above the higher levels.

And beyond, like a final backdrop, rose a titanic wall. It was from the crenellated parapets and battlements of that wall that Mr. Chambers felt the eyes peering at him, thousands of eyes glaring down with but a single purpose. As he continued to look, something else seemed to take form above that wall—a design this time, that swirled and writhed in the ribbons of radiance and rapidly coalesced into strange geometric features, without definite line or detail. A colossal face, a face of indescribable power and evil it was, staring down with malevolent composure.

Then the city and the face slid out of focus; the vision faded like a darkened magic lantern, and the grayness moved in again.

Mr. Chambers pushed open the door of his house. But he did not lock it. There was no need of locks—not any more.

A few coals of fire still smoldered in the grate and, going there, he stirred them up, raked away the ash, piled on more wood. The flames leaped merrily, dancing in the chimney's throat. Without removing his hat and coat, he sank exhausted in his favorite chair, closed his eyes, then opened them again.

He sighed with relief as he saw the room was unchanged. Everything was in its accustomed place: the clock, the lamp, the elephant ash tray, the marine print on the wall. Everything was as it should be. The clock measured the silence with its ticking; it chimed abruptly and the vase sent up its usual sympathetic vibration.

This was his room, he thought. Rooms acquire the personality of the person who lives in them, become a part of him. This was his world, his own private world, and as such it would be the last to go.

But how long could he maintain its existence?

Mr. Chambers stared at the marine print and for a moment a little breath of reassurance returned to him. *They* couldn't take this away. The rest of the world might dissolve because there was insufficient power of thought to retain its outward form. But this room was his. He alone had furnished it. He alone, since he had first planned the house's building, had lived here. This room would stay. It must stay on, it must. . . .

He crossed the room to the bookcase and stood staring at the second shelf with its single volume. His eyes shifted to the top shelf and swift terror gripped him.

For all the books were not there. A lot of books were not there! Only the most beloved, the most familiar ones. So the change already had started here! The unfamiliar books were gone and that fitted into the pattern—for it would be the least familiar things that would go first.

Wheeling, he stared across the room. Was it his imagination, or did the lamp on the table blur and begin to fade away? But as he stared at it, it became clear again, a solid, substantial thing.

For a moment real fear reached out and touched him with chilly fingers. He understood that this room no longer was proof against the thing that had happened out there on the street.

Or had it really happened? Might not all this exist within his own mind? Might not the street be as it always was, with laughing children and barking dogs? Might not the Red Star confectionery still exist, splashing the street with the red of its neon sign?

Could it be that he was going mad? He had heard whispers when he had passed, whispers the gossiping housewives had not intended him to hear. And he had heard the shouting of boys when he walked by. They thought him mad. Could he be really mad?

He was sure he was not mad. He knew that he perhaps was the sanest of all men who walked the earth. For he, and he alone, had foreseen this very thing. And the others had scoffed at him for it.

Somewhere else the children might be playing on a street. But it would be a different street. And the children undoubtedly would be different, too. For the matter of which the street and everything upon it had been formed would now be cast in a different mold, stolen by different minds in a different dimension.

Perhaps we shall come upon a day, far distant, when our plane, our world will dissolve beneath our feet and before our eyes as some stronger intelligence reaches out from the dimensional shadows of the very space we live in and wrests from us the matter which we know to be our own.

But there had been no need to wait for that distant day. Scant years after he had written those prophetic words the thing was happening. Man had played unwittingly into the hands of those other minds in the other dimension. Man had waged a war and war had bred a pestilence. And the whole vast cycle of events was but a detail of a cyclopean plan.

He could see it all now. By an insidious mass hypnosis, minions from that other dimension . . . or was it one supreme intelligence . . . had deliberately sown the seeds of dissension. The reduction of the world's mental power had been carefully planned with diabolic premeditation.

On impulse he suddenly turned, crossed the room and

opened the connecting door to the bedroom. He stopped on the threshold and a gasp forced its way to his lips.

There was no bedroom. Where his stolid four-poster and dresser had been there was grayish nothingness.

Like an automaton he turned again and paced to the hall door. Here, too, he found what he had expected. There was no hall, no familiar hat rack and umbrella stand.

Nothing . . .

Weakly, Mr. Chambers moved back to his chair in the corner.

"So here I am," he said, half aloud.

So there he was. Embattled in the last corner of the world that was left to him.

Perhaps there were other men like him, he thought. Men who stood at bay against the emptiness that marked the transition from one dimension to another. Men who had lived close to the things they loved, who had endowed those things with such substantial form by power of mind alone that they now stood out alone against the power of some greater mind.

The street was gone. The rest of his house was gone. This room still retained its form.

This room, he knew, would stay the longest. And when the rest of the room was gone, this corner with his favorite chair would remain. For this was the spot where he had lived for twenty years. The bedroom was for sleeping, the kitchen for eating. This room was for living. This was his last stand. These were the walls and floors and prints and lamps that had soaked up his will to make them walls and prints and lamps.

He looked out the window into a blank world. His neighbors' houses already were gone. They had not lived with them as he had lived with this room. Their interests had been divided, thinly spread; their thoughts had not been concentrated as his upon an area four blocks by three, or a room fourteen by twelve.

Staring through the window, he saw it again. The same vision he had looked upon before and yet different in an indescribable way. There was the city illumined in the sky. There were the elliptical towers and turrets, the cube-shaped domes and battlements. He could see with stereoscopic clarity the aerial bridges, the gleaming avenues sweeping on into infinitude. The vision was nearer this time, but the depth and proportion had changed, as if he were viewing it from two concentric angles at the same time.

And the face, the face of magnitude, of power, of cosmic craft and evil . . .

Mr. Chambers turned his eyes back into the room. The clock was ticking slowly, steadily. The grayness was stealing into the room. The table and radio were the first to go. They simply faded away and with them went one corner of the room.

Now as he sat there it did not seem queer to be without the table or the radio. It was as if it were something quite normal. Something one could expect to happen. Perhaps, if he thought hard enough, he could bring them back. But, after all, what was the use? One man, alone, could not stand off the irresistible march of nothingness. One man, all alone, simply could not.

He wondered what the elephant ash tray looked like in that other dimension. It certainly would not be an elephant ash tray, nor would the radio be a radio, for perhaps they did not have ash trays or radios or elephants in the invading dimension.

He wondered, as a matter of fact, what he himself would look like when he finally slipped into the unknown. For he was matter, too, just as the ash tray and radio were matter. He wondered if he would retain his individuality, if he still would be a person. Or would he merely be a thing?

There was one answer to all of that. He simply didn't know.

Nothingness advanced upon him, ate its way across the

room, stalking him as he sat in the chair underneath the lamp. He waited for it.

The room, or what was left of it, plunged into dreadful silence.

Mr. Chambers started. The clock had stopped. Funny . . . the first time in twenty years.

He leaped from his chair and then sat down again.

The clock hadn't stopped.

It wasn't there.

There was a tingling sensation in his feet.

DEAR DEVIL

Eric Frank Russell

*Not all creatures from beyond are invaders, or monsters, or
even dangerous . . . no matter how they may look. Some, like
the Martian explorer in the following story, might be poets
whose mission on Earth is one of love and understanding. But
they may have trouble convincing us of their good intentions,
if they look so frightening.*

*Eric Frank Russell has written many famous science-fiction
novels, including* Sinister Barrier *and* Dreadful Sanctuary,
*but his best-known story of all remains the following warm
and moving novelette.*

The first Martian vessel descended upon Earth with the
slow, stately fall of a grounded balloon. It did resemble a large
balloon in that it was spherical and had a strange buoyancy
out of keeping with its metallic construction. Beyond this
superficial appearance all similarity to anything Terrestrial
ceased.

There were no rockets, no crimson venturis, no external
projections other than several solaradiant distorting grids
which boosted the ship in any desired direction through the
cosmic field. There were no observation ports. All viewing
was done through a transparent band running right around
the fat belly of the sphere. The bluish, nightmarish crew was
assembled behind that band, surveying the world with great
multifaceted eyes.

They gazed through the band in utter silence as they examined this world which was Terra. Even if they had been capable of speech they would have said nothing. But none among them had a talkative faculty in any sonic sense. At this quiet moment none needed it.

The scene outside was one of untrammeled desolation. Scraggy blue-green grass clung to tired ground right away to the horizon scarred by ragged mountains. Dismal bushes struggled for life here and there, some with the pathetic air of striving to become trees as once their ancestors had been. To the right, a long, straight scar through the grass betrayed the sterile lumpiness of rocks at odd places. Too rugged and too narrow ever to have been a road, it suggested no more than the desiccating remnants of a long-gone wall. And over all this loomed a ghastly sky.

Captain Skhiva eyed his crew, spoke to them with his sign-talking tentacle. The alternative was contact telepathy, which required physical touch.

"It is obvious that we are out of luck. We could have done no worse had we landed on the empty satellite. However, it is safe to go out. Anyone who wishes to explore a little while may do so."

One of them gesticulated back at him. "Captain, don't you wish to be the first to step upon this world?"

"It is of no consequence. If anyone deems it an honor, he is welcome to it." He pulled the lever opening both air-lock doors. Thicker, heavier air crowded in and pressure went up a little. "Beware of overexertion," he warned as they went out.

Poet Fander touched him, tentacles tip to tip as he sent his thoughts racing through their nerve ends. "This confirms all that we saw as we approached. A stricken planet far gone in its death throes. What do you suppose caused it?"

"I have not the remotest idea. I would like to know. If it has been smitten by natural forces, what might they do to Mars?" His troubled mind sent its throb of worry up Fander's contacting tentacle. "A pity that this planet had not been far- ther out instead of closer in; we might then have observed the preceding phenomena from the surface of Mars. It is so difficult properly to view this one against the sun."

"That applies still more to the next world, the misty one," observed Poet Fander.

"I know it. I am beginning to fear what we may find there. If it proves to be equally dead, then we are stalled until we can make the big jump outward."

"Which won't be in our lifetimes."

"I doubt it," agreed Captain Skhiva. "We might move fast with the help of friends. We shall be slow—alone." He turned to watch his crew writhing in various directions across the grim landscape. "They find it good to be on firm ground. But what is a world without life and beauty? In a short time they will grow tired of it."

Fander said thoughtfully, "Nevertheless, I would like to see more of it. May I take out the lifeboat?"

"You are a songbird, not a pilot," reproved Captain Skhiva. "Your function is to maintain morale by entertaining us, not to roam around in a lifeboat."

"But I know how to handle it. Every one of us was trained to handle it. Let me take it that I may see more."

"Haven't we seen enough, even before we landed? What else is there to see? Cracked and distorted roads about to dis- solve into nothingness. Ages-old cities, torn and broken, crumbling into dust. Shattered mountains and charted forests and craters little smaller than those upon the moon. No sign of any superior life-form still surviving. Only the grass, the shrubs, and various animals, two- or four-legged, that flee at our approach. Why do you wish to see more?"

"There is poetry even in death," said Fander.

"Even so, it remains repulsive." Skhiva gave a little shiver. "All right. Take the lifeboat. Who am I to question the weird workings of the nontechnical mind?"

"Thank you, Captain."

"It is nothing. See that you are back by dusk." Breaking contact, he went to the lock, curled snakishly on its outer rim and brooded, still without bothering to touch the new world. So much attempted, so much done—for so poor reward.

He was still pondering it when the lifeboat soared out of its lock. Expressionlessly, his multifaceted eyes watched the energized grids change angle as the boat swung into a curve and floated away like a little bubble. Skhiva was sensitive to futility.

The crew came back well before darkness. A few hours were enough. Just grass and shrubs and child-trees straining to grow up. One had discovered a grassless oblong that once might have been the site of a dwelling. He brought back a small piece of its foundation, a lump of perished concrete, which Skhiva put by for later analysis.

Another had found a small, brown, six-legged insect, but his nerve ends had heard it crying when he picked it up, so hastily he had put it down and let it go free. Small, clumsily moving animals had been seen hopping in the distance, but all had dived down holes in the ground before any Martian could get near. All the crew were agreed upon one thing: the silence and solemnity of a people's passing was unendurable.

Fander beat the sinking of the sun by half a time-unit. His bubble drifted under a great, black cloud, sank to ship level, came in. The rain started a moment later, roaring down in frenzied torrents while they stood behind the transparent band and marveled at so much water.

After a while, Captain Skhiva told them, "We must accept what we find. We have drawn a blank. The cause of this world's condition is a mystery, to be solved by others with more time and better equipment. It is for us to abandon this graveyard and try the misty planet. We will take off early in the morning."

None commented, but Fander followed him to his room, made contact with a tentacle-touch.

"One could live here, Captain."

"I am not so sure of that." Skhiva coiled on his couch, suspending his tentacles on the various limb-rests. The blue sheen of him was reflected by the back wall. "In some places are rocks emitting alpha sparks. They are dangerous."

"Of course, Captain. But I can sense them and avoid them."

"*You?*" Skhiva stared up at him.

"Yes, Captain. I wish to be left here."

"What? In this place of appalling repulsiveness?"

"It has an all-pervading air of ugliness and despair," admitted Poet Fander. "All destruction is ugly. But by accident I have found a little beauty. It heartens me. I would like to seek its source."

"To what beauty do you refer?" Skhiva demanded.

Fander tried to explain the alien in nonalien terms.

"Draw it for me," ordered Skhiva.

Fander drew it, gave him the picture, said, "There!"

Gazing at it for a long time, Skhiva handed it back, mused awhile, then spoke along the other's nerves. "We are individuals with all the rights of individuals. As an individual, I don't think that picture sufficiently beautiful to be worth the tail tip of a domestic *arlan*. I will admit that it is not ugly, even that it is pleasing."

"But, Captain—"

"As an individual," Skhiva went on, "you have an equal right to your opinions, strange though they may be. If you really wish to stay, I cannot refuse you. I am entitled only to think you a little crazy." He eyed Fander again. "When do you hope to be picked up?"

"This year, next year, sometime, never."

"It may well be never," Skhiva reminded him. "Are you prepared to face that prospect?"

"One must always be prepared to face the consequences of one's own actions," Fander pointed out.

"True." Skhiva was reluctant to surrender. "But have you given the matter serious thought?"

"I am a nontechnical component. I am not guided by thought."

"Then by what?"

"By my desires, emotions, instincts. By my inward feelings."

Skhiva said fervently, "The twin moons preserve us!"

"Captain, sing me a song of home and play me the tinkling harp."

"Don't be silly. I have not the ability."

"Captain, if it required no more than careful thought, you would be able to do it?"

"Doubtlessly," agreed Skhiva, seeing the trap but unable to avoid it.

"There you are!" said Fander pointedly.

"I give up. I cannot argue with someone who casts aside the accepted rules of logic and invents his own. You are governed by notions that defeat me."

"It is not a matter of logic or illogic," Fander told him. "It is merely a matter of viewpoint. You see certain angles; I see others."

"For example?"

"You won't pin me down that way. I can find examples. For instance, do you remember the formula for determining the phase of a series-tuned circuit?"

"Most certainly."

"I felt sure you would. You are a technician. You have registered it for all time as a matter of technical utility." He paused, staring at Skhiva. "I know that formula, too. It was mentioned to me, casually, many years ago. It is of no use to me—yet I have never forgotten it."

"Why?"

"Because it holds the beauty of rhythm. It is a poem," Fander explained.

Skhiva sighed and said, "I don't get it."

"*One upon R into omega L minus one upon omega C,*" recited Fander. "A perfect hexameter." He showed his amusement as the other rocked back.

After a while, Skhiva remarked, "It could be sung. One could dance to it."

"Same with this." Fander exhibited his rough sketch. "This holds beauty. Where there is beauty there once was talent—may still be talent for all we know. Where talent abides is also greatness. In the realms of greatness we may find powerful friends. We *need* such friends."

"You win." Skhiva made a gesture of defeat. "We leave you to your self-chosen fate in the morning."

"Thank you, Captain."

That same streak of stubbornness which made Skhiva a worthy commander induced him to take one final crack at Fander shortly before departure. Summoning him to his room, he eyed the poet calculatingly.

"You are still of the same mind?"

"Yes, Captain."

"Then does it not occur to you as strange that I should be so content to abandon this planet if indeed it does hold the remnants of greatness?"

"No."

"Why not?" Skhiva stiffened slightly.

"Captain, I think you are a little afraid because you suspect what I suspect—that there was no natural disaster. They did it themselves, to themselves."

"We have no proof of it," said Skhiva uneasily.

"No, Captain." Fander paused there without desire to add more.

"*If* this is their own sad handiwork," Skhiva commented at

length, "what are our chances of finding friends among people so much to be feared?"

"Poor," admitted Fander. "But that—being the product of cold thought—means little to me. I am animated by warm hopes."

"There you go again, blatantly discarding reason in favor of an idle dream. Hoping, hoping, hoping—to achieve the impossible."

Fander said, "The difficult can be done at once; the impossible takes a little longer."

"Your thoughts make my orderly mind feel lopsided. Every remark is a flat denial of something that makes sense." Skhiva transmitted the sensation of a lugubrious chuckle. "Oh, well, we live and learn." He came forward, moving closer to the other. "All your supplies are assembled outside. Nothing remains but to bid you good-bye."

They embraced in the Martian manner. Leaving the lock, Poet Fander watched the big sphere shudder and glide up. It soared without sound, shrinking steadily until it was a mere dot entering a cloud. A moment later it had gone.

He remained there, looking at the cloud, for a long, long time. Then he turned his attention to the load-sled holding his supplies. Climbing onto its tiny, exposed front seat, he shifted the control that energized the flotation grids, let it rise a few feet. The higher the rise, the greater the expenditure of power. He wished to conserve power; there was no knowing how long he might need it. So at low altitude and gentle pace he let the sled glide in the general direction of the thing of beauty.

Later, he found a dry cave in the hill on which his objective stood. It took him two days of careful, cautious raying to square its walls, ceiling, and floor, plus half a day with a powered fan driving out silicate dust. After that, he stowed his supplies at the back, parked the sled near the front, set up a curtaining force-screen across the entrance. The hole in the hill was now home.

Slumber did not come easily that first night. He lay within the cave, a ropy, knotted thing of glowing blue with enormous, beelike eyes, and found himself listening for harps that played sixty million miles away. His tentacle ends twitched in involuntary search of the telepathic-contact songs that would go with the harps, and twitched in vain. Darkness grew deep, and all the world a monstrous stillness held. His hearing organs craved for the eventide flip-flop of sand frogs, but there were no frogs. He wanted the homely drone of night beetles, but none droned. Except for once when something faraway howled its heart at the moon, there was nothing, nothing.

In the morning he washed, ate, took out the sled, and explored the site of a small town. He found little to satisfy his curiosity, no more than mounds of shapeless rubble on ragged, faintly oblong foundations. It was a graveyard of long-dead domiciles, rotting, weedy, near to complete oblivion. A view from five hundred feet up gave him only one piece of information: the orderliness of outlines showed that these people had been tidy, methodical.

But tidiness is not beauty in itself. He came back to the top of his hill and sought solace with the thing that was beauty.

His explorations continued, not systematically as Skhiva would have performed them, but in accordance with his own mercurial whims. At times he saw many animals, singly or in groups, none resembling anything Martian. Some scattered at full gallop when his sled swooped over them. Some dived into groundholes, showing a brief flash of white, absurd tails. Others, four-footed, long-faced, sharp-toothed, hunted in gangs and bayed at him in concert with harsh, defiant voices.

On the seventieth day, in a deep, shadowed glade to the north, he spotted a small group of new shapes slinking along in single file. He recognized them at a glance, knew them so well that his searching eyes sent an immediate thrill of triumph into his mind. They were ragged, dirty, and no more than half grown, but the thing of beauty had told him what they were.

Hugging the ground low, he swept around in a wide curve that brought him to the farther end of the glade. His sled sloped slightly into the drop as it entered the glade. He could see them better now, even the soiled pinkishness of their thin legs. They were moving away from him, with fearful caution, but the silence of his swoop gave them no warning.

The rearmost one of the stealthy file fooled him at the last moment. He was hanging over the side of the sled, tentacles outstretched in readiness to snatch the end one with the wild mop of yellow hair when, responding to some sixth sense, his intended victim threw itself flat. His grasp shot past a couple of feet short, and he got a glimpse of frightened gray eyes two seconds before a dexterous side-tilt of the sled enabled him to make good his loss by grabbing the less wary next in line.

This one was dark haired, a bit bigger, and sturdier. It fought madly at his holding limbs while he gained altitude.

Then suddenly, realizing the queer nature of its bonds, it writhed around and looked straight at him. The result was unexpected; it closed its eyes and went completely limp.

It was still limp when he bore it into the cave, but its heart continued to beat and its lungs to draw. Laying it carefully on the softness of his bed, he moved to the cave's entrance and waited for it to recover. Eventually it stirred, sat up, gazed confusedly at the facing wall. Its black eyes moved slowly around, taking in the surroundings. Then they saw Fander. They widened tremendously, and their owner began to make high-pitched, unpleasant noises as it tried to back away through the solid wall. It screamed so much, in one rising throb after another, that Fander slithered out of the cave, right out of sight, and sat in the cold winds until the noises had died down.

A couple of hours later he made cautious reappearance to offer it food, but its reaction was so swift, hysterical, and heartrending that he dropped his load and hid himself as though the fear were his own. The food remained untouched for two full days. On the third, a little of it was eaten. Fander ventured within.

Although the Martian did not go near, the boy cowered away, murmuring, "Devil! Devil!" His eyes were red, with dark discoloration beneath them.

"Devil!" thought Fander, totally unable to repeat the alien word, but wondering what it meant. He used his sign-talking tentacle in a valiant effort to convey something reassuring. The attempt was wasted. The other watched its writhings half in fear, half with distaste, and showed complete lack of comprehension. He let the tentacle gently slither forward across the floor, hoping to make thought contact. The other recoiled from it as from a striking snake.

"Patience," he reminded himself. "The impossible takes a little longer."

Periodically he showed himself with food and drink, and nighttimes he slept fitfully on the coarse, damp grass beneath lowering skies—while the prisoner who was his guest enjoyed the softness of the bed, the warmth of the cave, the security of the force-screen.

Time came when Fander betrayed an unpoetic shrewdness by using the other's belly to estimate the ripeness of the moment. When, on the eighth day, he noted that his food offerings were now being taken regularly, he took a meal of his own at the edge of the cave, within plain sight, and observed that the other's appetite was not spoiled. That night he slept just within the cave, close to the force-screen, and as far from the boy as possible. The boy stayed awake late, watching him, but gave way to slumber in the small hours.

A fresh attempt at sign-talking brought no better results than before, and the boy still refused to touch his offered tentacle. All the same, he was gaining ground slowly. His overtures were still rejected, but with less revulsion. Gradually, ever so gradually, the Martian shape was becoming familiar, almost acceptable.

The sweet savor of success was Fander's in the middle of the next day. The boy had displayed several spells of emotional sickness during which he lay on his front with shaking body and emitted low noises while his eyes watered profusely. At such times the Martian felt strangely helpless and inadequate. On this occasion, during another attack, he took advantage of the sufferer's lack of attention and slid near enough to snatch away the box by the bed.

From the box he drew his tiny electroharp, plugged its connectors, switched it on, touched its strings with delicate affection. Slowly he began to play, singing an accompaniment deep inside himself. For he had no voice with which to sing out loud, but the harp sang it for him. The boy ceased his quiverings, sat up, all his attention upon the dexterous play of the tentacles and the music they conjured forth. And when he judged that at last the listener's mind was captured, Fander ceased with easy, quietening strokes, gently offered him the harp. The boy registered interest and reluctance. Careful not to move nearer, not an inch nearer, Fander offered it at full tentacle length. The boy had to take four steps to get it. He took them.

That was the start. They played together, day after day and sometimes a little into the night, while almost imperceptibly the distance between them was reduced. Finally they sat together, side by side, and the boy had not yet learned to laugh but no longer did he show unease. He could now extract a simple tune from the instrument and was pleased with his own aptitude in a solemn sort of way.

One evening as darkness grew, and the things that sometimes howled at the moon were howling again, Fander offered his tentacle tip for the hundredth time. Always the gesture had been unmistakable even if its motive was not clear, yet always it had been rebuffed. But now, now, five fingers curled around it in shy desire to please.

With a fervent prayer that human nerves would function just like Martian ones, Fander poured his thoughts through, swiftly, lest the warm grip be loosened too soon.

"Do not fear me. I cannot help my shape any more than you can help yours. I am your friend, your father, your mother. I need you as much as you need me."

The boy let go of him, began quiet, half-stifled whimpering noises. Fander put a tentacle on his shoulder, made little patting motions that he imagined were wholly Martian. For some inexplicable reason, this made matters worse. At his wits' end what to do for the best, what action to take that might be understandable in Terrestrial terms, he gave the problem up, surrendered to his instinct, put a long, ropy limb around the boy and held him close until the noises ceased and slumber came. It was then he realized the child he had taken was much younger than he had estimated. He nursed him through the night.

Much practice was necessary to make conversation. The boy had to learn to put mental drive behind his thoughts, for it was Fander's power to suck them out of him.

"What is your name?"

Fander got a picture of thin legs running rapidly.

He returned it in question form. "Speedy?"

An affirmative.

"What name do you call me?"

An unflattering montage of monsters.

"Devil?"

The picture whirled around, became confused. There was a trace of embarrassment.

"Devil will do," assured Fander. He went on. "Where are your parents?"

More confusion.

"You must have had parents. Everyone has a father and mother, haven't they? Don't you remember yours?"

Muddled ghost-pictures. Grown-ups leaving children. Grown-ups avoiding children, as if they feared them.

"What is the first thing you remember?"

"Big man walking with me. Carried me a bit. Walked again."

"What happened to him?"

"Went away. Said he was sick. Might make me sick too."

"Long ago?"

Confusion.

Fander changed his aim. "What of those other children—have they no parents either?"

"All got nobody."

"But you've got somebody now, haven't you, Speedy?"

Doubtfully. "Yes."

Fander pushed it farther. "Would you rather have me, or those other children?" He let it rest a moment before he added, "Or both?"

"Both," said Speedy with no hesitation. His fingers toyed with the harp.

"Would you like to help me look for them tomorrow and bring them here? And if they are scared of me, will you help them not to be afraid?"

"Sure!" said Speedy, licking his lips and sticking his chest out.

"Then," said Fander, "perhaps you would like to go for a walk today? You've been too long in this cave. Will you come for a walk with me?"

"Y'betcha!"

Side by side they went a short walk, one trotting rapidly along, the other slithering. The child's spirits perked up with this trip in the open; it was as if the sight of the sky and the feel of the grass made him realize at last that he was not ex-

actly a prisoner. His formerly solemn features became
animated, he made exclamations that Fander could not understand, and once he laughed at nothing for the sheer joy of it.
On two occasions he grabbed a tentacle tip in order to tell
Fander something, performing the action as if it were in every
way as natural as his own speech.

They got out the load-sled in the morning. Fander took the
front seat and the controls; Speedy squatted behind him with
hands gripping his harness belt. With a shallow soar, they
headed for the glade. Many small, white-tailed animals bolted
down holes as they passed over.

"Good for dinner," remarked Speedy, touching him and
speaking through the touch.

Fander felt sickened. Meateaters! It was not until a queer
feeling of shame and apology came back at him that he knew
the other had felt his revulsion. He wished he'd been swift to
blanket that reaction before the boy could sense it, but he
could not be blamed for the effect of so bald a statement taking him so completely unaware. However, it had produced
another step forward in their mutual relationship—Speedy desired his good opinion.

Within fifteen minutes they struck it lucky. At a point half
a mile south of the glade, Speedy let out a shrill yell and
pointed downward. A small, golden-haired figure was standing there on a slight rise, staring fascinatedly upward at the
phenomenon in the sky. A second tiny shape, with red but
equally long hair, was at the bottom of the slope gazing in
similar wonderment. Both came to their senses and turned to
flee as the sled tilted toward them.

Ignoring the yelps of excitement close behind him and the
pulls upon his belt, Fander swooped, got first one, then the
other. This left him with only one limb to right the sled and
gain height. If the victims had fought, he would have had his
work cut out to make it. They did not fight. They shrieked as
he snatched them and then relaxed with closed eyes.

The sled climbed, glided a mile at five hundred feet. Fander's attention was divided between his limp prizes, the controls, and the horizon when suddenly a thunderous rattling sounded on the metal base of the sled, the entire framework shuddered, a strip of metal flew from its leading edge and things made whining sounds toward the clouds.

"Old Graypate," bawled Speedy, jigging around but keeping away from the rim. "He's shooting at us."

The spoken words meant nothing to the Martian, and he could not spare a limb for the contact the other had forgotten to make. Grimly righting the sled, he gave it full power. Whatever damage it had suffered had not affected its efficiency; it shot forward at a pace that set the red and golden hair of the captives streaming in the wind. Perforce his landing by the cave was clumsy. The sled bumped down and lurched across forty yards of grass.

First things first. Taking the quiet pair into the cave, he made them comfortable on the bed, came out and examined the sled. There were half a dozen deep dents in its flat underside, two bright furrows angling across one rim. He made contact with Speedy.

"What were you trying to tell me?"

"Old Graypate shot at us."

The mind-picture burst upon him vividly and with electrifying effect: a vision of a tall, white-haired, stern-faced old man with a tubular weapon propped upon his shoulder while it spat fire upward. A white-haired old man! An adult!

His grip was tight on the other's arm. "What is this oldster to you?"

"Nothing much. He lives near us in the shelters."

Picture of a long, dusty concrete burrow, badly damaged, its ceiling marked with the scars of a lighting system that had rotted away to nothing. The old man living hermitlike at one end; the children at the other. The old man was sour, taciturn, kept the children at a distance, spoke to them seldom but was quick to respond when they were menaced. He had guns. Once he had killed many wild dogs that had eaten two children.

"People left us near the shelters because Old Graypate was there, and had guns," informed Speedy.

"But why does he keep away from children? Doesn't he like children?"

"Don't know." He mused a moment. "Once told us that old people could get very sick and make young ones sick—and then we'd all die. Maybe he's afraid of making us die." Speedy wasn't very sure about it.

So there was some much-feared disease around, something contagious, to which adults were peculiarly susceptible. Without hesitation they abandoned their young at the first onslaught, hoping that at least the children would live. Sacrifice after sacrifice that the remnants of the race might survive. Heartbreak after heartbreak as elders chose death alone rather than death together.

Yet Graypate himself was depicted as very old. Was this an exaggeration of the child-mind?

"I must meet Graypate."

"He will shoot," declared Speedy positively. "He knows by now that you took me. He saw you take the others. He will wait for you and shoot."

"We will find some way to avoid that."

"How?"

"When these two have become my friends, just as you have become my friend, I will take all three of you back to the shelters. You can find Graypate for me and tell him that I am not as ugly as I look."

"I don't think you're ugly," denied Speedy.

The picture Fander got along with that gave him the weirdest sensation of pleasure. It was of a vague, shadowy but distorted body with a clear human face.

The new prisoners were female. Fander knew it without being told because they were daintier than Speedy and had the warm, sweet smell of females. That meant complications. Maybe they were mere children, and maybe they lived together in the shelter, but he was permitting none of that while they were in his charge. Fander might be outlandish by other standards but he had a certain primness. Forthwith he cut another and smaller cave for Speedy and himself.

Neither of the girls saw him for two days. Keeping well out of their sight, he let Speedy take them food, talk to them, prepare them for the shape of the thing to come. On the third day he presented himself for inspection at a distance. Despite forewarnings they went sheet-white, clung together, but uttered no distressing sounds. He played his harp a little while, withdrew, came back in the evening and played for them again.

Encouraged by Speedy's constant and self-assured flow of propaganda, one of them grasped a tentacle tip next day. What came along the nerves was not a picture so much as an ache, a desire, a childish yearning. Fander backed out of the cave, found wood, spent the whole night using the sleepy Speedy as a model, and fashioned the wood into a tiny, jointed semblance of a human being. He was no sculptor, but he possessed a natural delicacy of touch, and the poet in him ran through his limbs and expressed itself in the model. Making a thorough job of it, he clothed it in Terrestrial fashion, colored its face, fixed upon its features the pleasure-grimace that humans call a smile.

He gave her the doll the moment she awakened in the morning. She took it eagerly, hungrily, with wide, glad eyes. Hugging it to her unformed bosom, she crooned over it—and he knew that the strange emptiness within her was gone.

Though Speedy was openly contemptuous of this manifest waste of effort, Fander set to and made a second mannikin. It did not take quite as long. Practice on the first had made him swifter, more dexterous. He was able to present it to the other child by midafternoon. Her acceptance was made with shy grace, she held the doll close as if it meant more than the whole of her sorry world. In her thrilled concentration upon the gift, she did not notice his nearness, his closeness, and when he offered a tentacle, she took it.

He said simply, "I love you."

Her mind was too untrained to drive a response, but her great eyes warmed.

Fander sat on the grounded sled at a point a mile east of the glade and watched the three children walk hand in hand toward the hidden shelters. Speedy was the obvious leader, hurrying them onward, bossing them with the noisy assurance of one who has been around and considers himself sophisticated. In spite of this, the girls paused at intervals to turn and wave to the ropy, bee-eyed thing they'd left behind. And Fander dutifully waved back, always using his signaling tentacle because it had not occurred to him that any tentacle would serve.

They sank from sight behind a rise of ground. He remained on the sled, his multifaceted gaze going over his surroundings or studying the angry sky now threatening rain. The ground was a dull, dead gray-green all the way to the horizon. There was no relief from that drab color, not one shining patch of white, gold, or crimson such as dotted the meadows of Mars. There was only the eternal gray-green and his own brilliant blueness.

Before long a sharp-faced, four-footed thing revealed itself in the grass, raised its head and howled at him. The sound was an eerily urgent wail that ran across the grasses and moaned into the distance. It brought others of its kind, two, ten, twenty. Their defiance increased with their numbers until there was a large band of them edging toward him with lips drawn back, teeth exposed. Then there came a sudden and undetectable flock command that caused them to cease their slinking and spring forward like one, slavering as they came. They did it with the hungry, red-eyed frenzy of animals motivated by something akin to madness.

Repulsive though it was, the sight of creatures craving for meat—even strange blue meat—did not bother Fander. He slipped a control a notch, the flotation grids radiated, the sled soared twenty feet. So calm and easy an escape so casually performed infuriated the wild dog pack beyond all measure. Arriving beneath the sled, they made futile springs upward, fell back upon one another, bit and slashed each other, leaped again and again. The pandemonium they set up was a compound of snarls, yelps, barks, and growls, the ferocious expressions of extreme hate. They exuded a pungent odor of dry hair and animal sweat.

Reclining on the sled in a maddening pose of disdain, Fander let the insane ones rave below. They raced around in tight circles shrieking insults at him and biting each other. This went on for some time and ended with a spurt of ultrarapid cracks from the direction of the glade. Eight dogs fell dead. Two flopped and struggled to crawl away. Ten yelped in agony, made off on three legs. The unharmed ones flashed away to some place where they could make a meal of the escaping limpers. Fander lowered the sled.

Speedy stood on the rise with Graypate. The latter restored his weapon to the crook of his arm, rubbed his chin thoughtfully, ambled forward.

Stopping five yards from the Martian, the old Earthman again massaged his chin whiskers, then said, "It sure is the darnedest thing, just the darnedest thing!"

"No use talking *at* him," advised Speedy. "You've got to touch him, like I told you."

"I know, I know." Graypate betrayed a slight impatience. "All in good time. I'll touch him when I'm ready." He stood there, gazing at Fander with eyes that were very pale and very sharp. "Oh, well, here goes." He offered a hand.

Fander placed a tentacle end in it.

"Jeepers, he's cold," commented Graypate, closing his grip. "Colder than a snake."

"He isn't a snake," Speedy contradicted fiercely.

"Ease up, ease up—I didn't say he is." Graypate seemed fond of repetitive phrases.

"He doesn't feel like one, either," persisted Speedy, who had never felt a snake and did not wish to.

Fander boosted a thought through. "I come from the fourth planet. Do you know what that means?"

"I ain't ignorant," snapped Graypate aloud.

"No need to reply vocally. I receive your thoughts exactly as you receive mine. Your responses are much stronger than the boy's, and I can understand you easily."

"Humph!" said Graypate to the world at large.

"I have been anxious to find an adult because the children can tell me little. I would like to ask questions. Do you feel inclined to answer questions?"

"It depends," answered Graypate, becoming leery.

"Never mind. Answer them if you wish. My only desire is to help you."

"Why?" asked Graypate, searching around for a percentage.

"We need intelligent friends."

"Why?"

"Our numbers are small, our resources poor. In visiting this world and the misty one we've come near to the limit of our ability. But with assistance we could go farther. I think that if we could help you a time might come when you could help us."

Graypate pondered it cautiously, forgetting that the inward workings of his mind were wide open to the other. Chronic suspicion was the keynote of his thoughts, suspicion based on life experiences and recent history. But inward thoughts ran both ways, and his own mind detected the clear sincerity in Fander's.

So he said, "Fair enough. Say more."

"What caused all this?" inquired Fander, waving a limb at the world.

"War," said Graypate. "The last war we'll ever have. The entire place went nuts."

"How did that come about?"

"You've got me there." Graypate gave the problem grave consideration. "I reckon it wasn't just any one thing; it was a multitude of things sort of piling themselves up."

"Such as?"

"Differences in people. Some were colored differently in their bodies, others in their ideas, and they couldn't get along. Some bred faster than others, wanted more room, more food. There wasn't any more room or more food. The world was full, and nobody could shove in except by pushing another out. My old man told me plenty before he died, and he always maintained that if folk had had the hoss-sense to keep their numbers down, there might not—"

"Your old man?" interjected Fander. "Your father? Didn't all this occur in your own lifetime?"

"It did not. I saw none of it. I am the son of the son of a survivor."

"Let's go back to the cave," put in Speedy, bored with this silent contact talk. "I want to show him our harp."

They took no notice, and Fander went on, "Do you think there might be a lot of others still living?"

"Who knows?" Graypate was moody about it. "There isn't any way of telling how many are wandering around the other side of the globe, maybe still killing each other, or starving to death, or dying of the sickness."

"What sickness is this?"

"I couldn't tell what it is called." Graypate scratched his

head confusedly. "My old man told me a few times, but I've long forgotten. Knowing the name wouldn't do me any good, see? He said his father told him that it was part of the war, it got invented and was spread deliberately—and it's still with us."

"What are its symptoms?"

"You go hot and dizzy. You get black swellings in the armpits. In forty-eight hours you're dead. Old ones get it first. The kids then catch it unless you make away from them mighty fast."

"It is nothing familiar to me," said Fander, unable to recognize cultured bubonic. "In any case, I'm not a medical expert." He eyed Graypate. "But you seem to have avoided it."

"Sheer luck," opined Graypate. "Or maybe I can't get it. There was a story going around during the war that some folk might develop immunity to it, durned if I know why. Could be that I'm immune, but I don't count on it."

"So you keep your distance from these children?"

"Sure." He glanced at Speedy. "I shouldn't really have come along with this kid. He's got a lousy chance as it is without me increasing the odds."

"That is thoughtful of you," Fander put over softly. "Especially seeing that you must be lonely."

Graypate bristled and his thought flow became aggressive. "I ain't grieving for company. I can look after myself, like I have done since my old man went away to curl up by himself. I'm on my own feet. So's every other guy."

"I believe that," said Fander. "You must pardon me—I'm a stranger here myself. I judged you by my own feelings. Now and again I get pretty lonely."

"How come?" demanded Graypate, staring at him. "You ain't telling me they dumped you and left you, on your own?"

"They did."

"Man!" exclaimed Graypate fervently.

Man! It was a picture resembling Speedy's conception, a vision elusive in form but firm and human in face. The oldster was reacting to what he considered a predicament rather than a choice, and the reaction came on a wave of sympathy.

Fander struck promptly and hard. "You see how I'm fixed. The companionship of wild animals is nothing to me. I need someone intelligent enough to like my music and forget my looks, someone intelligent enough to—"

"I ain't so sure we're that smart," Graypate chipped in. He let his gaze swing morbidly around the landscape. "Not when I see this graveyard and think of how it looked in Grandpop's days."

"Every flower blooms from the dust of a hundred dead ones," answered Fander.

"What are flowers?"

It shocked the Martian. He had projected a mind-picture of a trumpet lily, crimson and shining, and Graypate's brain had juggled it around, uncertain whether it was fish, flesh, or fowl.

"Vegetable growths, like these." Fander plucked half a dozen blades of blue-green grass. "But more colorful, and sweet-scented." He transmitted the brilliant vision of a mile-square field of trumpet lilies, red and glowing.

"Glory be!" said Graypate. "We've nothing like those."

"Not here," agreed Fander. "Not here." He gestured toward the horizon. "Elsewhere may be plenty. If we got together we could be company for each other, we could learn things from each other. We could pool our ideas, our efforts, and search for flowers far away—also for more people."

"Folk just won't get together in large bunches. They stick to each other in family groups until the plague breaks them up. Then they abandon the kids. The bigger the crowd, the bigger the risk of someone contaminating the lot." He leaned on his gun, staring at the other, his thought-forms shaping themselves in dull solemnity. "When a guy gets hit, he goes away and takes it on his own. The end is a personal contract between him and his God, with no witnesses. Death's a pretty private affair these days."

"What, after all these years? Don't you think that by this time the disease may have run its course and exhausted itself?"

"Nobody knows—and nobody's gambling on it."

"I would gamble," said Fander.

"You ain't like us. You mightn't be able to catch it."

"Or I might get it worse, and die more painfully."

"Mebbe," admitted Graypate, doubtfully. "Anyway, you're looking at it from a different angle. You've been dumped on your ownsome. What've you got to lose?"

"My life," said Fander.

Graypate rocked back on his heels, then said, "Yes, sir, that is a gamble. A guy can't bet any heavier than that." He rubbed his chin whiskers as before. "All right, all right, I'll take you up on that. You come right here and live with us." His grip tightened on his gun, his knuckles showing white. "On this understanding: The moment you feel sick you get out fast, and for keeps. If you don't, I'll bump you and drag you away myself, even if that makes me get it too. The kids come first, see?"

The shelters were far roomier than the cave. There were eighteen children living in them, all skinny with their prolonged diet of roots, edible herbs, and an occasional rabbit. The youngest and most sensitive of them ceased to be terrified of Fander after ten days. Within four months his slithering shape of blue ropiness had become a normal adjunct to their small, limited world.

Six of the youngsters were males older than Speedy, one of them much older but not yet adult. He beguiled them with his harp, teaching them to play, and now and again giving them ten-minute rides on the load-sled as a special treat. He made dolls for the girls and queer, cone-shaped little houses for the dolls, and fan-backed chairs of woven grass for the houses. None of these toys were truly Martian in design, and none were Terrestrial. They represented a pathetic compromise within his imagination; the Martian notion of what Terrestrial models might have looked like had there been any in existence.

But surreptitiously, without seeming to give any less attention to the younger ones, he directed his main efforts upon the six older boys and Speedy. To his mind, these were the hope of the world—and of Mars. At no time did he bother to ponder that the nontechnical brain is not without its virtues, or that there are times and circumstances when it is worth dropping the short view of what is practicable for the sake of the long view of what is remotely possible. So as best he could he concentrated upon the elder seven, educating them through the dragging months, stimulating their minds, encouraging their curiosity, and continually impressing upon them the idea that fear of disease can become a folk-separating dogma unless they conquered it within their souls.

He taught them that death is death, a natural process to be accepted philosophically and met with dignity—and there were times when he suspected that he was teaching them nothing, he was merely reminding them, for deep within their growing minds was the ancestral strain of Terrestrialism that had mulled its way to the same conclusions ten or twenty thousands of years before. Still, he was helping to remove this disease block from the path of the stream, and was driving child logic more rapidly toward adult outlook. In that respect he was satisfied. He could do little more.

In time, they organized group concerts, humming or making singing noises to the accompaniment of the harp, now and again improvising lines to suit Fander's tunes, arguing out the respective merits of chosen words until by process of elimination they had a complete song. As songs grew to a repertoire and singing grew more adept, more polished, Old

Graypate displayed interest, came to one performance, then another, until by custom he had established his own place as a one-man audience.

One day the eldest boy, who was named Redhead, came to Fander and grasped a tentacle tip. "Devil, may I operate your food machine?"

"You mean you would like me to show you how to work it?"

"No, Devil, I know how to work it." The boy gazed self-assuredly into the other's great bee eyes.

"Then how is it operated?"

"You fill its container with the tenderest blades of grass, being careful not to include roots. You are equally careful not to turn a switch before the container is full and its door completely closed. You then turn the red switch for a count of two hundred eighty, reverse the container, turn the green switch for a count of forty-seven. You then close both switches, empty the container's warm pulp into the end molds and apply the press until the biscuits are firm and dry."

"How have you discovered all this?"

"I have watched you make biscuits for us many times. This morning, while you were busy, I tried it myself." He extended a hand. It held a biscuit. Taking it from him, Fander examined it. Firm, crisp, well shaped. He tasted it. Perfect.

Redhead became the first mechanic to operate and service a Martian lifeboat's emergency premasticator. Seven years later, long after the machine had ceased to function, he managed to repower it, weakly but effectively, with dust that gave forth alpha sparks. In another five years he had improved it, speeded it up. In twenty years he had duplicated it and had all the know-how needed to turn out premasticators on a large scale. Fander could not have equaled this performance for, as a nontechnician, he'd no better notion than the average Terrestrial of the principles upon which the machine worked, neither did he know what was meant by radiant digestion or protein enrichment. He could do little more than urge Redhead along and leave the rest to whatever inherent genius the boy possessed—which was plenty.

In similar manner, Speedy and two youths named Blacky and Bigears took the load-sled out of his charge. On rare occasions, as a great privilege, Fander had permitted them to take up the sled for one-hour trips, alone. This time they were gone from dawn to dusk. Graypate mooched around, gun under arm, another smaller one stuck in his belt, going frequently to the top of a rise and scanning the skies in all directions. The delinquents swooped in at sunset, bringing with them a strange boy.

Fander summoned them to him. They held hands so that his touch would give him simultaneous contact with all three.

"I am a little worried. The sled has only so much power. When it is all gone there will be no more."

They eyed each other aghast.

"Unfortunately, I have neither the knowledge nor the ability to energize the sled once its power is exhausted. I lack the wisdom of the friends who left me here—and that is my shame." He paused, watched them dolefully, then went on. "All I do know is that its power does not leak away. If not used much, the reserves will remain for many years." Another pause before he added, "And in a few years you will be men."

Blacky said, "But, Devil, when we are men we'll be much heavier, and the sled will use so much more power."

"How do you know that?" Fander put it sharply.

"More weight, more power to sustain it," opined Blacky with the air of one whose logic is incontrovertible. "It doesn't need thinking out. It's obvious."

Very slowly and softly, Fander told him, "You'll do. May the twin moons shine upon you someday, for I know you'll do."

"Do what, Devil?"

"Build a thousand sleds like this one, or better—and explore the whole world."

From that time onward they confined their trips strictly to one hour, making them less frequently than of yore, spending more time poking and prying around the sled's innards.

Graypate changed character with the slow reluctance of the aged. Leastways, as two years, then three, rolled past, he came gradually out of his shell, was less taciturn, more willing to mix with those swiftly growing up to his own height. Without fully realizing what he was doing, he joined forces with Fander, gave the children the remnants of Earthly wisdom passed down from his father's father. He taught the boys how to use the guns of which he had as many as eleven, some maintained mostly as a source of spares for others. He took them shell hunting; digging deep beneath rotting foundations into stale, half-filled cellars in search of ammunition not too far corroded for use.

"Guns ain't no use without shells, and shells don't last forever."

Neither do buried shells. They found not one.

Of his own wisdom Graypate stubbornly withheld but a single item until the day when Speedy and Redhead and Blacky chivvied it out of him. Then, like a father facing the hangman, he gave them the truth about babies. He made no comparative mention of bees because there were no bees, nor of flowers because there were no flowers. One cannot analogize the nonexistent. Nevertheless he managed to explain the matter more or less to their satisfaction, after which he mopped his forehead and went to Fander.

"These youngsters are getting too nosy for my comfort. They've been asking me how kids come along."

"Did you tell them?"

"I sure did." He sat down, staring at the Martian, his pale gray eyes bothered. "I don't mind giving in to the boys when

I can't beat 'em off any longer, but I'm durned if I'm going to tell the girls."

Fander said, "I have been asked about this many a time before. I could not tell much because I was by no means certain whether you breed precisely as we breed. But I told them how *we* breed."

"The girls too?"

"Of course."

"Jeepers!" Graypate mopped his forehead again. "How did they take it?"

"Just as if I'd told them why the sky is blue or why water is wet."

"Must've been something in the way you put it to them," opined Graypate.

"I told them it was poetry between persons."

Throughout the course of history, Martian, Venusian, or Terrestrial, some years are more noteworthy than others. The twelfth one after Fander's marooning was outstanding for its series of events, each of which was pitifully insignificant by cosmic standards but loomed enormously in this small community life.

To start with, on the basis of Redhead's improvements to the premasticator, the older seven—now bearded men—contrived to repower the exhausted sled and again took to the air for the first time in forty months. Experiments showed that the Martian load-carrier was now slower, could bear less weight, but had far longer range. They used it to visit the ruins of distant cities in search of metallic junk suitable for the building of more sleds, and by early summer they had constructed another, larger than the original, clumsy to the verge of dangerousness, but still a sled.

On several occasions they failed to find metal but did find people, odd families surviving in undersurface shelters, clinging grimly to life and passed-down scraps of knowledge. Since all these new contacts were strictly human to human, with no weirdly tentacled shape to scare off the parties of the second part, and since many were finding fear of plague more to be endured than their terrible loneliness, many families returned with the explorers, settled in the shelters, accepted Fander, added their surviving skills to the community's riches.

Thus local population grew to seventy adults and four hundred children. They compounded with their plague fear by spreading through the shelters, digging through half-wrecked and formerly unused expanses, and moving apart to form twenty or thirty lesser communities, each one of which could be isolated should death reappear.

Growing morale born of added strength and confidence in numbers soon resulted in four more sleds, still clumsy but slightly less dangerous to manage. There also appeared the first rock house above ground, standing four-square and solidly under the gray skies, a defiant witness that mankind still considered itself a cut above the rats and rabbits. The community presented the house to Blacky and Sweetvoice, who had announced their desire to associate. An adult who claimed to know the conventional routine spoke solemn words over the happy couple before many witnesses, while Fander attended the groom as best Martian.

Toward summer's end Speedy returned from a solo sled trip of many days, brought with him one old man, one boy, and four girls, all of strange, outlandish countenance. They were yellow in complexion, had black hair, black, almond-shaped eyes, and spoke a language that none could understand. Until these newcomers had picked up the local speech, Fander had to act as interpreter, for his mind-pictures and theirs were independent of vocal sounds. The four girls were quiet, modest, and very beautiful. Within a month Speedy had married one of them whose name was a gentle clucking sound that meant Precious Jewel Ling.

After this wedding, Fander sought Graypate, placed a tentacle tip in his right hand. "There were differences between the man and the girl, distinctive features wider apart than any we know upon Mars. Are these some of the differences that caused your war?"

"I dunno. I've never seen one of these yellow folk before. They must live mighty far off." He rubbed his chin to help his thoughts along. "I only know what my old man told me and his old man told him. There were too many folk of too many different sorts."

"They can't be all that different if they can fall in love."

"Mebbe not," agreed Graypate.

"Supposing most of the people still in this world could assemble here, breed together, and have less different children; the children breed others still less different. Wouldn't they eventually become all much the same—just Earth-people?"

"Mebbe so."

"All speaking the same language, sharing the same culture? If they spread out slowly from a central source, always in contact by sled, continually sharing the same knowledge, same progress, would there be any room for new differences to arise?"

"I dunno," said Graypate evasively. "I'm not so young as I used to be, and I can't dream as far ahead as I used to do."

"It doesn't matter so long as the young ones can dream it." Fander mused a moment. "If you're beginning to think yourself a back number, you're in good company. Things are getting somewhat out of hand as far as I'm concerned. The onlooker sees the most of the game, and perhaps that's why I'm more sensitive than you to a certain peculiar feeling."

"To what feeling?" inquired Graypate, eyeing him.

"That Terra is on the move once more. There are now many people where there were few. A house is up and more are to follow. They talk of six more. After the six they will talk of sixty, then six hundred, then six thousand. Some talk of planning to haul up sunken conduits and using them to pipe water from the northward lake. Sleds are being built, and force-screens likewise. Children are being taught. Less and less is being heard of your plague, and so far no more have died of it. I feel a dynamic surge of energy and ambition and genius which may grow with appalling rapidity until it becomes a mighty flood. I feel that I, too, am a back number."

"Bunk!" said Graypate. He spat on the ground. "If you dream often enough, you're bound to have a bad one once in a while."

"Perhaps it is because so many of my tasks have been taken over and done better than I was doing them. I have failed to seek new tasks. Were I a technician I'd have discovered a dozen by now. Reckon this is as good a time as any to turn to a job with which you can help me."

"What is that?"

"A long, long time ago I made a poem. It was for the beautiful thing that first impelled me to stay here. I do not know exactly what its maker had in mind, nor whether my eyes see it as he wished it to be seen, but I have made a poem to express what I feel when I look upon his work."

"Humph!" said Graypate, not very interested.

"There is an outcrop of solid rock beneath its base which I can shave smooth and use as a plinth on which to inscribe my words. I would like to put them down twice—in the script of Mars and the script of Earth." Fander hesitated a moment, then went on. "Perhaps this is presumptuous of me, but it is many years since I wrote for all to read—and my chance may never come again."

Graypate said, "I get the idea. You want me to put down your notions in our writing so you can copy it."

"Yes."

"Give me your stylus and pad." Taking them, Graypate squatted on a rock, lowering himself stiffly, for he was feeling the weight of his years. Resting the pad on his knees, he held the writing instrument in his right hand while his left continued to grasp a tentacle tip. "Go ahead."

He started drawing thick, laborious marks as Fander's mind-pictures came through, enlarging the letters and keeping them well separated. When he had finished he handed the pad over.

"Asymmetrical," decided Fander, staring at the queer letters and wishing for the first time that he had taken up the study of Earth-writing. "Cannot you make this part balance with that, and this with this?"

"It's what you said."

"It is your own translation of what I said. I would like it better balanced. Do you mind if we try again?"

They tried again. They made fourteen attempts before Fander was satisfied with the perfunctory appearance of letters and words he could not understand.

Taking the paper, he found his ray gun, went to the base rock of the beautiful thing and sheared the whole front to a flat, even surface. Adjusting his beam to cut a V-shaped channel one inch deep, he inscribed his poem on the rock in long, unpunctuated lines of neat Martian curlicues. With less confidence and much greater care, he repeated the verse in Earth's awkward, angular hieroglyphics. The task took him quite a time, and there were fifty people watching him when he finished. They said nothing. In utter silence they looked at the poem and at the beautiful thing, and were still standing there brooding solemnly when he went away.

One by one the rest of the community visited the site next day, going and coming with the air of pilgrims attending an ancient shrine. All stood there a long time, returned without comment. Nobody praised Fander's work, nobody damned it, nobody reproached him for alienizing something wholly Earth's. The only effect—too subtle to be noteworthy—was a greater and still growing grimness and determination that boosted the already swelling Earth-dynamic.

A plague scare came in the fourteenth year. Two sleds had brought back families from afar, and within a week of their arrival the children sickened, became spotted.

Metal gongs sounded the alarm, all work ceased, the affected section was cut off and guarded, the majority prepared to flee. It was a threatening reversal of all the things for which many had toiled so long; a destructive scattering of the tender roots of new civilization.

Fander found Graypate, Speedy, and Blacky, armed to the teeth, facing a drawn-faced and restless crowd.

"There's most of a hundred folk in that isolated part," Graypate was telling them. "They ain't all got it. Maybe they won't get it. If they don't, it ain't so likely you'll go down either. We ought to wait and see. Stick around a bit."

"Listen who's talking," invited a voice in the crowd. "If you weren't immune, you'd have been planted thirty-forty years ago."

"Same goes for near everybody," snapped Graypate. He glared around, his gun under one arm, his pale gray eyes bellicose. "I ain't much use at speechifying, so I'm just saying flatly that nobody goes before we know whether this really is the plague." He hefted his weapon in one hand, held it forward. "Anyone fancy himself at beating a bullet?"

The heckler in the audience muscled his way to the front. He was a swarthy man of muscular build, and his dark eyes looked belligerently into Graypate's. "While there's life, there's hope. If we beat it, we live to come back, when it's safe to come back, if ever—and you know it. So I'm calling your bluff, see?" Squaring his shoulders, he began to walk off.

Graypate's gun already was halfway up when he felt the touch of Fander's tentacle on his arm. He lowered the weapon, called after the escapee.

"I'm going into that cut-off section and the Devil is going with me. We're running into things, not away from them. I never did like running away." Several of the audience

fidgeted, murmured approval. He went on, "We'll see for
ourselves just what's wrong. We mightn't be able to put it
right, but we'll find out what's the matter."

The walker paused, turned, eyed him, eyed Fander, and
said, "You can't do that."

"Why not?"

"You'll get it yourself—and a heck of a lot of use you'll be
dead and stinking."

"What, and me immune?" cracked Graypate, grinning.

"The Devil will get it," hedged the other.

Graypate was about to retort, "What do you care?" but altered it slightly in response to Fander's contacting thoughts.
He said, more softly, "Do you *care?*"

It caught the other off balance. He fumbled embarrassedly
within his own mind, avoided looking at the Martian, said
lamely, "I don't see reason for any guy to take risks."

"He's taking them, because *he* cares," Graypate gave back.
"And I'm taking them because I'm too old and useless to give
a darn."

With that, he stepped down, marched stubbornly toward
the isolated section, Fander slithering by his side, tentacle in
hand. The one who wished to flee stayed put, staring after
them. The crowd shuffled uneasily, seemed in two minds
whether to accept the situation and stick around, or whether
to rush Graypate and Fander and drag them away. Speedy
and Blacky made to follow the pair but were ordered off.

No adult sickened; nobody died. Children in the affected
sector went one after another through the same routine of
liverishness, high temperature, and spots, until the epidemic
of measles had died out. Not until a month after the last case
had been cured by something within its own constitution did
Graypate and Fander emerge.

The innocuous course and eventual disappearance of this
suspected plague gave the pendulum of confidence a push,

swinging it farther. Morale boosted itself almost to the verge of arrogance. More sleds appeared, more mechanics serviced them, more pilots rode them. More people flowed in; more oddments of past knowledge came with them.

Humanity was off to a flying start with the salvaged seeds of past wisdom and the urge to do. The tormented ones of Earth were not primitive savages, but surviving organisms of a greatness nine-tenths destroyed but still remembered, each contributing his mite of know-how to restore at least some of those things that had been boiled away in atomic fires.

When, in the twentieth year, Redhead duplicated the premasticator, there were eight thousand stone houses standing around the hill. A community hall seventy times the size of a house, with a great green dome of copper, reared itself up on the eastward fringe. A dam held the lake to the north. A hospital was going up in the west. The nuances and energies and talents of fifty races had built this town and were still building it. Among them were ten Polynesians and four Icelanders and one lean, dusky child who was the last of the Seminoles.

Farms spread wide. One thousand heads of Indian corn rescued from a sheltered valley in the Andes had grown to ten thousand acres. Water buffaloes and goats had been brought from afar to serve in lieu of the horses and sheep that would never be seen again—and no man knew why one species survived while another did not. The horses had died; the water buffaloes lived. The canines hunted in ferocious packs; the felines had departed from existence. The small herbs, some tubers, and a few seedy things could be rescued and cultivated for hungry bellies; but there were no flowers for the hungry mind. Humanity carried on, making do with what was available. No more than that could be done.

Fander was a back number. He had nothing left for which to live but his songs and the affection of the others. In everything but his harp and his songs the Terrans were way ahead of him. He could do no more than give of his own affection in return for theirs and wait with the patience of one whose work is done.

At the end of that year they buried Graypate. He died in his sleep, passing with the undramatic casualness of one who ain't much use at speechifying. They put him to rest on a knoll behind the community hall, and Fander played his mourning song, and Precious Jewel, who was Speedy's wife, planted the grave with sweet herbs.

In the spring of the following year Fander summoned Speedy and Blacky and Redhead. He was coiled on a couch, blue and shivering. They held hands so that his touch would speak to them simultaneously.

"I am about to undergo my *amafa.*"

He had great difficulty in putting it over in understandable thought-forms, for this was something beyond their Earthly experience.

"It is an unavoidable change of age during which my kind must sleep undisturbed." They reacted as if the casual reference to his kind was a strange and startling revelation, a new aspect previously unthought of. He continued, "I must be left alone until this hibernation has run its natural course."

"For how long, Devil?" asked Speedy, with anxiety.

"It may stretch from four of your months to a full year, or—"

"Or what?" Speedy did not wait for a reassuring reply. His agile mind was swift to sense the spice of danger lying far back in the Martian's thoughts. "Or it may never end?"

"It may never," admitted Fander, reluctantly. He shivered again, drew his tentacles around himself. The brilliance of his blueness was fading visibly. "The possibility is small, but it is there."

Speedy's eyes widened and his breath was taken in a short gasp. His mind was striving to readjust itself and accept the appalling idea that Fander might not be a fixture, permanent, established for all time. Blacky and Redhead were equally aghast.

"We Martians do not last forever," Fander pointed out, gently. "All are mortal, here and there. He who survives his *amafa* has many happy years to follow, but some do not survive. It is a trial that must be faced as everything from beginning to end must be faced."

"But—"

"Our numbers are not large," Fander went on. "We breed slowly and some of us die halfway through the normal span. By cosmic standards we are a weak and foolish people much in need of the support of the clever and the strong. You are the clever and strong. Whenever my people visit you again, or any other still stranger people come, always remember that you are clever and strong."

"We are strong," echoed Speedy, dreamily. His gaze swung around to take in the thousands of roofs, the copper dome, the thing of beauty on the hill. "We are strong."

A prolonged shudder went through the ropy, bee-eyed creature on the couch.

"I do not wish to be left here, an idle sleeper in the midst of life, posing like a bad example to the young. I would rather rest within the little cave where first we made friends and grew to know and understand each other. Wall it up and fix a door for me. Forbid anyone to touch me or let the light of day fall upon me until such time as I emerge of my own accord." Fander stirred sluggishly, his limbs uncoiling with noticeable lack of sinuousness. "I regret I must ask you to carry me there. Please forgive me; I have left it a little late and cannot . . . cannot . . . make it by myself."

Their faces were pictures of alarm, their minds bells of sorrow. Running for poles, they made a stretcher, edged him onto it, bore him to the cave. A long procession was following by the time they reached it. As they settled him comfortably and began to wall up the entrance, the crowd watched in the same solemn silence with which they had looked upon his verse.

He was already a tightly rolled ball of dull blueness, with filmed eyes, when they fitted the door and closed it, leaving him to darkness and slumber. Next day a tiny, brown-skinned man with eight children, all hugging dolls, came to the door. While the youngsters stared huge-eyed at the door, he fixed upon it a two-word name in metal letters, taking great pains over his self-imposed task and making a neat job of it.

The Martian vessel came from the stratosphere with the slow, stately fall of a grounding balloon. Behind the transparent band its bluish, nightmarish crew were assembled and looking with great, multifaceted eyes at the upper surface of the clouds. The scene resembled a pink-tinged snowfield beneath which the planet still remained concealed.

Captain Rdina could feel this as a tense, exciting moment even though his vessel had not the honor to be the first with such an approach. One Captain Skhiva, now long retired, had done it many years before. Nevertheless, this second venture retained its own exploratory thrill.

Someone stationed a third of the way around the vessel's belly came writhing at top pace toward him as their drop brought them near to the pinkish clouds. The oncomer's signaling tentacle was jiggling at a seldom-used rate.

"Captain, we have just seen an object swoop across the horizon."

"What sort of an object?"

"It looked like a gigantic load-sled."

"It couldn't have been."

"No, Captain, of course not—but that is exactly what it appeared to be."

"Where is it now?" demanded Rdina, gazing toward the side from which the other had come.

"It dived into the mists below."

"You must have been mistaken. Long-standing anticipation can encourage the strangest delusions." He stopped a moment as the observation band became shrouded in the vapor of a cloud. Musingly, he watched the gray wall of fog slide upward as his vessel continued its descent. "That old report says definitely that there is nothing but desolation and wild animals. There is no intelligent life except some fool of a minor poet whom Skhiva left behind, and twelve to one he's dead by now. The animals may have eaten him."

"Eaten him? Eaten *meat?*" exclaimed the other, thoroughly revolted.

"Anything is possible," assured Rdina, pleased with the extreme to which his imagination could be stretched. "Except a load-sled. That was plain silly."

At which point he had no choice but to let the subject drop for the simple and compelling reason that the ship came out of the base of the cloud, and the sled in question was floating alongside. It could be seen in complete detail, and even their own instruments were responding to the powerful output of its numerous flotation grids.

The twenty Martians aboard the sphere sat staring beeeyed at this enormous thing that was half the size of their own vessel, and the forty humans on the sled stared back with equal intentness. Ship and sled continued to descend side by side, while both crews studied each other with dumb fascination that persisted until simultaneously they touched ground.

It was not until he felt the slight jolt of landing that Captain Rdina recovered sufficiently to look elsewhere. He saw the houses, the green-domed building, the thing of beauty poised upon its hill, the many hundreds of Earth-people streaming out of their town and toward his vessel.

None of these queer, two-legged life forms, he noted, betrayed the slightest sign of revulsion or fear. They galloped to the tryst with a bumptious self-confidence that would still be evident anyplace the other side of the cosmos.

It shook him a little, and he kept saying to himself, again and again, "They're not scared—why should you be? They're not scared—why should you be?"

He went out personally to meet the first of them, suppressing his own apprehensions and ignoring the fact that many of them bore weapons. The leading Earthman, a big-built, spade-bearded two-legger, grasped his tentacle as to the manner born.

There came a picture of swiftly moving limbs. "My name is Speedy."

The ship emptied itself within ten minutes. No Martian would stay inside who was free to smell new air. Their first visit, in a slithering bunch, was to the thing of beauty. Rdina stood quietly looking at it, his crew clustered in a half-circle around him, the Earth-folk a silent audience behind.

It was a great rock statue of a female of Earth. She was broad-shouldered, full-bosomed, wide-hipped, and wore voluminous skirts that came right down to her heavy-soled shoes. Her back was a little bent, her head a little bowed, and her face was hidden in her hands, deep in her toil-worn hands. Rdina tried in vain to gain some glimpse of the tired features behind those hiding hands. He looked at her a long while before his eyes lowered to read the script beneath, ignoring the Earth-lettering, running easily over the flowing Martian curlicues:

> Weep, my country, for your songs asleep,
> The ashes of your homes, your tottering towers.
> Weep, my country, O, my country, weep!
> For birds that cannot sing, for vanished flowers,
> The end of everything,
> The silenced hours.
> Weep! my country.

There was no signature. Rdina mulled it through many minutes, while the others remained passive. Then he turned to Speedy, pointed to the Martian script.

"Who wrote this?"

"One of your people. He is dead."

"Ah!" said Rdina. "That songbird of Skhiva's. I have forgotten his name. I doubt whether many remember it. He was only a very small poet. How did he die?"

"He ordered us to enclose him for some long and urgent sleep he must have, and—"

"The *amafa*," put in Rdina, comprehendingly. "And then?"

"We did as he asked. He warned us that he might never come out." Speedy gazed at the sky, unconscious that Rdina was picking up his sorrowful thoughts. "He has been there nearly two years and has not emerged." The eyes came down to Rdina. "I don't know whether you can understand me, but he was one of us."

"I think I understand." Rdina was thoughtful. He asked, "How long is this period you call nearly two years?"

They managed to work it out between them, translating it from Terran to Martian time-terms.

"It is long," pronounced Rdina. "Much longer than the usual *amafa,* but not unique. Occasionally, for no known reason, someone takes even longer. Besides, Earth is Earth and Mars is Mars." He became swift, energetic as he called to one of his crew. "Physician Traith, we have a prolonged *amafa* case. Get your oils and essences and come with me." When the other had returned, he said to Speedy, "Take us to where he sleeps."

Reaching the door to the walled-up cave, Rdina paused to look at the names fixed upon it in neat but incomprehensible letters. They read: DEAR DEVIL.

"What do those mean?" asked Physician Traith, pointing.

"Do not disturb," guessed Rdina carelessly. Pushing open

the door, he let the other enter first, closed it behind him to keep all others outside.

They reappeared an hour later. The total population of the city had congregated outside the cave to see the Martians. Rdina wondered why they had not permitted his crew to satisfy their natural curiosity, since it was unlikely that they would be more interested in other things—such as the fate of one small poet. Ten thousand eyes were upon them as they came into the sunlight and fastened the cave's door. Rdina made contact with Speedy, gave him the news.

Stretching himself in the light as if reaching toward the sun, Speedy shouted in a voice of tremendous gladness that all could hear.

"He will be out again within twenty days."

At that, a mild form of madness seemed to overcome the two-leggers. They made pleasure-grimaces, piercing mouth-noises, and some went so far as to beat each other.

Twenty Martians felt like joining Fander that same night. The Martian constitution is peculiarly susceptible to emotion.